"No, wait..." Nick said.

She was about to ask what he wanted, when the descent of his head made it perfectly clear.

It was as if he knew how important this kiss was to her, she thought, as his lips lightly tasted hers, then drew back, then settled more firmly to coax a response that had waited just for him to awaken it.

He nuzzled her neck for a moment, mumbling incoherent words that sounded terribly sexy to Meg. Her breath caught each time his lips touched her skin.

"I've been wanting to kiss you like that ever since I met you," he said softly.

"You have?"

"Yes. And guess what?"

Meg trembled slightly at the raspy quality of his voice. "What?"

"I don't think I can stop at just one."

Dear Reader,

Warning! Don't read April's terrific lineup of Silhouette Romance titles *unless* you're ready to catch spring fever!

The FABULOUS FATHERS series continues with Suzanne Carey's *Dad Galahad.* Ned Balfour, the story's hero, is all a modern knight should be—and *more.* Ned gallantly marries pregnant Jenny McClain to give her child a name. But he never expects the powerful emotions that come with being a father. *And* Jenny's husband.

Garrett Scott, the hero of *Who's That Baby?* by Kristin Morgan, is a father with a mysterious past. He's a man on the run, determined to protect his daughter. Then Garrett meets Whitney Arceneaux, a woman whose warmth and beauty tempt him to share his secret—and his heart.

Laurie Paige's popular ALL-AMERICAN SWEETHEARTS trilogy concludes this month with a passionate battle of wills in *Victoria's Conquest.* Jason Broderick fell in love with Victoria Broderick years ago—the day she married his late cousin. Now that Victoria is free and needs help, Jason will give her just about anything she wants. Anything *but* his love.

Rounding out the list, there's the sparkling, romantic mix-up of Patricia Ellis's *Sorry, Wrong Number* and Maris Soule's delightful and moving love story, *Lyon's Pride.* One of your favorite authors, Marie Ferrarella blends just the right touch of heartfelt emotion, warmth and humor in *The Right Man.*

In the coming months, look for more books by your favorite authors, including Diana Palmer, Elizabeth August, Phyllis Halldorson and many more.

Happy reading from all of us at Silhouette!

Anne Canadeo
Senior Editor

SORRY, WRONG NUMBER
Patricia Ellis

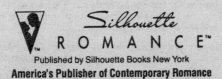

Silhouette
R O M A N C E™
Published by Silhouette Books New York
America's Publisher of Contemporary Romance

For Mildred Strickland . . . and not just because of
the hint. Mimi, if I didn't have your best friend for
my mother, I'd want you.
Love, Doozy.

SILHOUETTE BOOKS
300 E. 42nd St., New York, N.Y. 10017

SORRY, WRONG NUMBER

Copyright © 1993 by Valerie Mangrum

ISBN: 0-373-08931-7

First Silhouette Books printing April 1993

All the characters in this book have no existence outside the
imagination of the author and have no relation whatsoever to
anyone bearing the same name or names. They are not even
distantly inspired by any individual known or unknown to the
author, and all incidents are pure invention.

®: Trademark used under license and registered in the United
States Patent and Trademark Office and in other countries.

Printed in the U.S.A.

Books by Patricia Ellis

Silhouette Romance

Sweet Protector #684
Champagne and Wildflowers #799
Pillow Talk #820
Keeping Up with the Joneses #846
Sorry, Wrong Number #931

PATRICIA ELLIS

was "dramatized" at a very young age and never recovered. After a life spent in and out of institutions—of higher education—she now holds two degrees in theatre arts and acts whenever she's allowed, which is never often enough. She is a stubborn believer in happy endings, so it was predictable that this optimist, who loves Shakespearean comedy (but is constantly trying to find a way to help Romeo and Juliet out of that mess they're in), would fall under the spell of romance novels. Several years later, between theatre degrees, she decided to try writing one of her favorite kinds of books. Imagine her delight when an obviously brilliant and perspicacious editor at Silhouette bought that book. Imagine a standing ovation on opening night, and you've got the picture. Now, writing and acting may not be the most secure professions to pursue, but—hands down—they're the most creatively fulfilling. Not to mention the most fun.

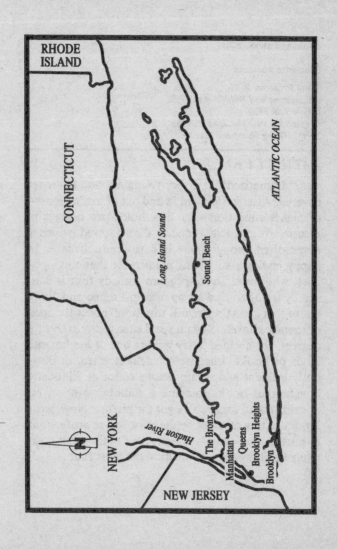

Chapter One

"That's something I didn't expect to see."

Meg Porter looked over at the man who'd just spoken. She'd been standing over the jukebox, trying to decide what to play. "What?"

Bill Ferguson, a frequenter of the remodeled tavern they were in, didn't speak. He merely shifted his eyes toward the door.

Meg turned and looked over her shoulder. The front door was wide open, a man was holding it for a woman, and when she stepped out and linked her arm with his, the door shut behind them. Staring with disbelieving blue eyes, Meg abandoned the jukebox and sank down on a bench beside Bill.

"Am I wrong," Bill inquired, "or was that guy with you when you came in?"

The flush of humiliation staining her pale cheeks, Meg nodded. "You aren't wrong. We were together. He said he was going to the rest room."

Bill shook his head. "What a jerk. Look, Meg, I don't know you real well. You've only been in here—what, three or four times? But I know him. Greg Bayer is usually an okay guy, but he's got some kind of blind spot when it comes to Jerri Jacobs. Last year he had a thing for her, then, when she married another guy, he moped around for a while, but then seemed okay. I heard she broke up with her husband," he finished lamely.

Meg couldn't believe she was sitting at a table in a bar she didn't particularly like, talking with a man she didn't really know, about another man who'd just dumped her without so much as a goodbye.

"Don't worry about it, Bill," Meg shrugged. "I didn't really know Greg all that well. We only started going out about two weeks ago."

Bill shook his head and sipped his beer. "Still a crummy thing to do."

Sighing raggedly as she laid money on the table for her drink, Meg rose. "On that, Bill, we are in complete agreement."

She left the tavern and pulled up the collar of her coat to ward off the chilly wind. She could have called a cab, but her apartment was only six blocks away. It wasn't such a big deal.

Kicking at the few patches of snow left on the ground, Meg tried not to think about Greg Bayer. It really shouldn't hurt at all, she thought dispassionately. Her love life had been the pits for...

"Forever!" Meg snapped. If anyone noticed the dark-haired young woman muttering to herself, they ignored her. Ah, New York, Meg thought. Or, more correctly, Ah, Brooklyn Heights.

By the time she'd let herself into her tiny studio apartment, Meg vacillated between anger at Greg for being such a swine and anger at herself for feeling so hurt. Tears of anger and embarrassment shimmered in her eyes as she flung her coat off and draped it haphazardly over her coatrack.

She marched over and jerked her kitchen window shade down. Her new neighbor across the fire escape was a man, and she didn't want to see his face, even if it was handsome.

The telephone rang and Meg snarled at it. "Go away. I don't want to talk to anybody. I don't want anybody to know that I've just been dumped by a guy I didn't even really like."

But the phone continued to ring. Snatching it from its cradle, Meg practically barked into the receiver. "What?"

Silence greeted her, then a tentative, "Heddo? Addison?"

An unfamiliar male voice with the classic Brooklyn accent—plus some sort of additional strange nasal twang—greeted her. Meg decided that it didn't matter whether she knew this guy or not. He was a man, and tonight, men were creeps.

"No, this isn't Addison, and even if he were here, I wouldn't tell you, because you're a man, and right now, all men are to be scorned and spurned by any intelligent female."

More silence. "Uh, soddy, lady. Is dis 555-5682?"

"No, it isn't. It's 5683."

After she'd said it, she realized that she probably shouldn't have, because now, whoever she was talking to would have her number in case he were a pervert and wanted to call back and harass her.

"Soddy, I was trying to cawd my sister."

Meg frowned. "You have a sister named Addison?"

The voice on the other end sighed. "Not Addison. Addison."

About to hang up on an obviously disturbed person, Meg paused, thinking. "Oh, Allison."

"Right. Soddy ip I disturbed you. And, ip you don't mide my saying so, you shoudn't gib out your real pone number to strange men."

Meg gripped the receiver, wishing it was the throat of this ridiculous-sounding male she was listening to. "Don't tell me what to do. I can give my phone number to anyone I want, strange or not. And, if you ask me, all men are strange. It's just that some are sneakier about letting women know it."

"Whassa madder, lady? Some guy dump ya?"

She considered screaming into the phone, but didn't. After all, he was right. Infuriatingly, maddeningly, masculinely right. "Yes, as a matter of fact, some guy did. Thank you very much for inquiring. I hope you die of a horrible, male-oriented disease."

With that, she slammed the phone down and marched over to her kitchen, which only took three steps, since her kitchen was, more or less, part of her living room. Which was, more or less, part of her bedroom.

Jerking open a cabinet, she pulled out a coffee mug and set it on the counter. She was just reaching for her teakettle when the telephone rang again. Meg closed her eyes and took a deep breath. What now?

"Hello?"

"Listen, lady, I'm soddy ip I hurd your peelings."

Meg fell into the armchair next to the telephone table and dropped her head into her hand. "You didn't hurt my feelings. Someone else did. And what's wrong with your voice?"

"I hab a code."

"Oh. Well, eat some chicken soup and drink lots of orange juice. Did you take any aspirin?"

For all her ranting about men, Meg Porter had a maternal streak that wouldn't die. Even strange men who were no more than wrong numbers got her concern.

"Dat's why I was cawdding Addison. I ran out of ordange juice. But I cawd you by bistake and den I insudded you."

Meg shook her head, the sheer insanity of the situation causing her to smile. "You didn't insult me. It was another man who did that. You just happened to call at the wrong time, and be a man."

"Nod all men are creeps."

"I know that," Meg sighed. "It just seems as if all the ones who are are the only ones I ever go out with. I know I'm not gorgeous, but I would think that, just once, a normal man, with a normal life, would want to go out on a normal date with me. And not tell me he's going to the rest room and then leave with another woman!"

"Oh, dat's low," the voice said in sympathy. "I hope dat you habn't been going out wid dis guy for long."

"No, I haven't. Only a few times, as a matter of fact. It's just the fact that anybody would do that to anybody that's hard to swallow."

Meg suddenly realized that she was telling a total stranger things about her life that she wouldn't tell her best friends.

But there was a certain rightness about that, she thought. There were no pitying looks or awkward attempts to cheer her up from an unknown entity with a Brooklyn accent and a plugged-up nose.

"Yeah, I guess you're righd," he was saying. "And whadda you mean, you're not gorgeous? Whadda you look like?"

"What kind of a question is that?" Meg gasped. Then she frowned. "Are you going to get perverted and start asking me what I'm wearing?"

"Don'd be ridiculous, lady. I was just woddering why you diddunt think you were good looking."

"I didn't say that," Meg objected. "I guess I'm attractive enough. But I'm not beautiful. My face is too round and I have freckles and my thighs are too fat."

She heard laughing and then a coughing fit. "Soddy, lady, but women always say dings like dat. And id's only odder women who nodice dings like dat. And eben ip you're right...why don'd you go to a gym and work out? I think freckles are cude, and I got no idea whad you mean about your face."

Meg smiled ruefully at herself and had to admit that her mystery caller was right. She had no real reason to gripe. She was attractive, even pretty. But she'd never be beautiful. At least not according to high-fashion or Hollywood standards. "Okay, okay. I guess you're right. I hate to admit it, but you've actually made me feel better. Thanks."

"Hey, doe problem. Not all wrong numbers hab to be intrusions."

"Right. And I want you to call Allison and get her to bring you some orange juice."

"Okay. Talk to you again sometime, lady."

"Sure," Meg said. "Anytime."

"You did *what?*"

Meg smiled at her assistant manager. The bookstore was just about to open and Shawn had tsk-tsked her way through Meg's story about Greg, only to gasp when Meg told her about her telephone conversation.

"I said I let a wrong number be my therapist for a while. He was very nice, even though he did have a cold and it was hard to understand what he was saying sometimes."

"You're crazy," Shawn insisted. "Who knows what kind of nut he was? Now he could call you anytime and make obscene suggestions."

Meg laughed. "He had the chance to get obscene last night, and didn't. What do you expect him to do? Call back later and say he forgot to talk dirty? I know it was weird, but it was sort of nice. It was nice being able to talk to someone without fear of future repercussions. I don't know him, and he doesn't know me. I didn't have to worry about what he would think of me if I said something stupid."

Shawn unlocked the front door to the store and turned the Closed sign around to read Open. "Well, I suppose that after what you'd been through, you weren't thinking too clearly, anyway. If I were you, I'd go punch Greg Bayer in the nose. No, better yet, send him some of those dead black roses or something disgusting like a rat. There's this company in the Village that will deliver all sorts of weird things." Her brown eyes danced. "A rat for a rat. I like it."

Meg chuckled as she set up the cash registers for the day. "There is a certain amount of poetic justice in those sorts of things, but to tell you the truth, I wouldn't want to give him the satisfaction of thinking that I cared that much. And I don't."

"Are you sure?"

"Yes," Meg stated positively. "You may scoff at my anonymous caller, but he did a lot for my self-esteem last night. In fact, I think I'm going to start an exercise program."

A customer came in, but just started browsing, so Shawn turned back to Meg. "Really? That's great. I'm ashamed to admit that I've slacked off on my aerobics myself. Not enough self-motivation. But when you go with somebody else, it's more fun. And besides, summer is approaching, and I need to get into shape."

Meg nodded. "Me, too. My thighs and I have come to an impasse. They want to stay the way they are, and I want them to shrink."

"You don't have to lose any weight," Shawn said. "I think you have a complex about your body. And I don't think it has anything to do with your thighs."

"I was a chubby teenager. And while I might not really need to lose weight," Meg admitted, leveling a look at Shawn that dared her to say anything about the only part of her body that was, in Meg's opinion, disproportionately large, "I do need to exercise and tone up my muscles. Letting everything go soft and flabby isn't a real confidence builder. Exercising regularly is supposed to make you feel better about yourself. Right?"

"Right," Shawn agreed.

"I don't know about aerobics, though." Meg hesitated. "I think I'd get too bored with doing the same thing all the time."

Shawn nodded. "That's true, and part of the reason why I've stopped going as often as I should. Maybe we should try something different. Like swimming, or jogging two days a week and aerobics three days."

Meg grimaced. "That's an awful lot of exercising."

"Not really. And there was a doctor on one of the morning shows last week who said that to get any real benefit, you have to exercise at least four days a week."

"Well, all right. But forget jogging."

Shawn sighed. "You could wear a good support bra."

Meg's jaw was set stubbornly. "Easy for you to say. No jogging."

"Okay, okay. How about swimming?"

To Meg, it wasn't much better a choice. "I don't know. I've never been much of a swimmer. Are those our only options? Can't we just walk?"

"Sure. But it takes longer and you go farther to get the same workout."

"So? I'm in no hurry."

Shawn's brown eyes twinkled. "Or... we could take up bicycling."

"In Brooklyn? Talk about your dangerous sports."

"Lots of people ride in the parks or on the Promenade," Shawn insisted. "There are those special paths just for bikes. And I'd bet Nick would be willing to give us a discount."

Meg frowned. "I don't know."

"What do you mean, you don't know? Nick Morgan is very cute, very muscled and very single. What could you possibly have against him?"

"Nothing, I guess. I don't like the way he looks at me."

Shawn made a frustrated sound in her throat that caused the browsing customer to look up with a frown. "The way he looks at you? What does he do? Does he leer, does he smirk? Does he drool?"

"No, of course not," Meg retorted. "He just... I don't know... let's just say he has a hard time looking me in the eye."

"You mean he's had the nerve to look at your chest."

Meg's eyes shot to the customer, who apparently hadn't heard anything. Then she turned her gaze back to Shawn, whose expression was challenging. "I don't like it when men stare at me like that. It makes it perfectly clear that they aren't interested in me as a person, just in the size of my... endowments."

Shawn rolled her eyes disgustedly. "Have you looked at yourself lately, Meg? I mean, most women would probably kill to have 'endowments' like yours. In fact, some of them pay doctors good money to—"

"Yeah, yeah," Meg cut in. "You've sung this song before."

"What is it with you? Your weight is in proportion with your height, you don't have cellulite, you don't have little rolls of fat that bulge out around your waistband. So your breasts are a little larger than the average woman's. As complaints go, that one isn't likely to generate a lot of sympathy from your sisters. Especially if they're like me and got the short end of the stick.''

Meg looked around hastily. "Geez, Shawn, keep your voice down."

She could just feel people staring at her. She remembered how she'd been stared at when she was in high school. She'd fibbed just a little to Shawn. Meg had never been a chubby teenager. Just too voluptuous at an early age. Girls had envied her then, and their stares had been discomfiting. But the stares of the girls had been nothing compared to the stares of the boys.

Thinking back to her high school days always depressed her, and Meg wondered why she couldn't just forget the crude remarks and ogling stares and put it behind her. As she'd grown older, her body had lengthened and filled out in other places, so that her chest wasn't quite the attention-getter it had been then. At least, that's what Meg tried to tell herself.

She was just a little bigger than average, according to clothes manufacturers. A whole size bigger than average, she thought with an internal sigh.

"Yes, buddy, this is the place to be to meet babes. You definitely went into the right business. Look around you, what do you see?"

Nick blinked and squinted slightly. "I see two big, hairy men checking out mountain bikes."

"Morgan, I realize that you've been ill recently, but I know you're not dead. Over there."

Nick followed Gary's gaze to look through a maze of bicycle tire spokes to see three young women trying on helmets.

"Uh-huh. Nice."

Gary snorted. "Nice? These women are better than nice, Nicky. They have well-developed muscle tone and sleek—"

"Yeah, yeah, I get it," Nick laughed. "I understand where you're coming from, but you forget that I work here and see these kinds of women every day."

"You don't have to rub it in," Gary complained. "And what are you saying, that you've become immune to beautiful women with beautiful bodies?"

"No, of course not. But it does take somebody special to really get my attention. For you, all she has to have are two X chromosomes and a little mascara."

"Go on," Gary drawled, "amuse yourself at my expense. But I don't suppose you've run across one of these special bodies recently?"

Nick shrugged, and Gary pounced. "You have. Whoa, boy, she must be something. Who is she?"

"She manages the bookstore next door. I only talked to her once, but I don't think she's interested."

"Really? How unusual. Probably just playing hard to get. But a bookstore? An intellectual type? Nick, this is so unlike you."

They were interrupted briefly as the two men who had been looking at the mountain bikes asked Nick several questions. One of them then ordered a special bike. As they were leaving, they held the door open for two women coming into the store.

"Look out, look out," Gary said abruptly. "Check it out, two possible biker babes dead ahead."

"You know, Gary, if any of the women you were trying to meet ever heard you refer to them as 'babes' or 'chicks,' you'd never get another date as long as you live."

Gary just grinned. "I know. That's why, when they're in earshot, I am most respectful and call them ladies."

About to make a few remarks to Gary about sincerity, Nick found himself staring at the women his friend had pointed out instead. He recognized them and waved. One smiled and waved back. The other refused to meet his eyes and looked away. For the second time, Nick wondered what her problem was.

"That's my next-door neighbor," Nick said, his voice low.

Gary shook his head. "It just isn't fair. My next-door neighbor is a butcher named Murray. So, what's her name? Who's her friend? For that matter, which one is the neighbor?"

"The one with the fantastic—"

"Fantastic is right."

"—legs."

Gary seemed confused. "Oh, right, them, too. Good grief, Nick, is she attached to a guy named Killer? Why haven't you made your move? Turned on the old Morgan charm?"

Nick watched as the two women halted just out of earshot and entered into a somewhat heated discussion. "Her name is Meg Porter and her friend is Shawn Something. And I don't think she likes me. Meg, that is. We met about a week ago and she seemed sort of chilly, if you get my drift."

"Cold? With a body like that? No way. Wait a minute. You opened this store two weeks ago. And you've only met her once?"

Nick nodded. "I've been busy."

"I know, I know. Your budding bicycle empire has been taking up all of your time. I, too, am a successful young gogetter, but never would I let something like my career interfere with the pursuit of the greatest pleasures of life. I thought we were in accord on this most vital of matters. Maybe your cold has affected more than your head. I know it's affected your voice. Your accent is showing."

Nick grimaced. "I know. It comes back every time I get a cold. It was worse yesterday. I could barely understand myself. But I took my medicine, and Allison brought me some orange juice. It's almost gone."

He thought about the wrong number he'd called the night before and smiled. That girl had been so upset she'd talked to a wrong number for ten minutes. But she'd cared enough to tell him to take care of himself. That was what made him wonder what she was like. There weren't many people who had that kind of compassion for a total stranger.

"I think they're coming this way," Gary announced. "For a minute there, I thought they were about to leave."

Nick just chuckled at his friend and stepped around him, prepared to greet Meg and Shawn. Gary was right about his putting business before pleasure lately. It was just that operating the two bicycle shops he owned was taking up most of his time. Especially now that spring was just about here and people were bringing their bikes in to be serviced. It was also the peak buying time. It was a surprise even to himself to admit that he hadn't been out on a date in more than a month. And it was horrifyingly longer than that since he'd—

"Hi," Shawn said as she and Meg neared the counter Nick and Gary were leaning against.

Nick nodded and smiled. "Hello. Nice to see you again. This is Gary Pearson, a friend of mine. Gary, this is Meg Porter and Shawn... I'm sorry, I don't remember your last name."

"It's Harryld. And I'm not sure you ever heard it, so don't feel bad. It's nice to meet you, Gary."

Nick turned to Meg. "Did you just close up for the day?"

He made sure to exert extra effort to control his accent and the faint residuals from his stuffed-up nose. No one seemed to notice, so he must have been doing a good job.

"Yes, we did," she said.

"And we decided to come over here because Meg and I have decided to take up bicycling."

Nick's eyes cut back to Meg, who was watching somewhat patiently, and he got the impression that it had been Shawn's idea to take up bicycling.

"Really? Well, lucky for me I just opened up next door to you."

Gary grinned at both Meg and Shawn. "Yeah, Nick here is a regular entrepreneur. He has another store, in Queens, you know."

"Do you?" Meg asked, her blue eyes finally meeting his.

"Yeah. I wanted to open up around here first, but I couldn't get the right location until now."

"It's difficult," she agreed. "People are always calling the store and asking if we're moving anytime soon. There used to be a barbershop here. But the man who owned it retired about four months ago."

Nick frowned slightly. What was it about her that gave him a feeling of déjà vu? He'd only met her last week…and he knew that he'd never forget someone like Meg Porter. Forcing his mind back to the conversation, he said, "That was when I bought it. It took a while to renovate it, although the upstairs didn't need as much work as this did," Nick added, gesturing at his retail space.

"Upstairs?"

Gary nodded at Shawn's question. "Yeah. There's a two-bedroom apartment above this place. Very nice. So he got a store and an apartment for one price. Pretty shrewd, huh?"

Shawn smiled and looked at Meg. "Meg probably thinks so, since she lives above the bookstore. Since your fire escapes are practically touching, I suppose you two must see a lot of each other."

Meg frowned at her friend. "I wouldn't say a lot."

Nick wasn't sure, but it seemed almost as if Meg glared at Shawn, and Shawn just ignored it. At this point, it seemed as if his best course of action was to take Meg's side. "No, not a lot. Although I suppose if you ever needed help, you could yell and I'd hear you."

That seemed to fluster Meg a bit, but she just said, "I guess. Thanks for the thought."

Now what had he done? Nick couldn't decide if she was shy or a snob. So he tried again. "It's convenient, though, isn't it? Living above your work? Saves me a lot on rent."

Meg nodded. "Me, too. My apartment is owned by the bookstore chain, so I have to rent it from them, but they give me a break. Of course, it's only a little studio. Not nearly as big as yours."

Someone cleared their throat and Nick, who'd let his eyes slip appreciatively down Meg's curvy body and long, long legs, jerked his eyes upward and found her glaring at him. "Not as big? That's too bad." What had he done now? If looks could kill, that icy glare of hers would have laid him low from frostbite.

"Anyway," Shawn said, "we were wondering if you could show us some bikes. Nothing too expensive or fancy, since we're just doing it for exercise."

"Shawn, maybe we should think about this more," Meg began.

"No, we shouldn't," Shawn said firmly. "We talked about this all day, and now we're going to stop talking and start riding."

Nick still didn't understand what had happened to make Meg an iceberg. He walked over to a stand of inexpensive five- and ten-speeds and pointed out the merits of the different types.

"How often do you plan to ride?"

Shawn laughed. "That probably depends on how much we like it. Most likely, two or three times a week."

Nick nodded. "You know, you might want to consider getting secondhand bikes. Then, if you decide you really like cycling, you could buy something better."

"Do you sell used bikes, as well as new ones?"

Nick nodded at Shawn. "Yes. I buy several older bikes a month and recondition them."

"That's interesting. We sell new and used books. Of course, we call them rare books."

Gary laughed with Shawn, Nick smiled at Meg, and Meg's smile looked forced.

"Anyway," Nick continued. "The used bikes are over here."

He led Meg and Shawn, with Gary trailing, across to the opposite corner where several bikes stood in a stand.

"These are used?" Shawn ran her hand over a seat.

"Yes. But they have new tires and seats, and most of them have new paint jobs."

"Well, I like this blue one," Shawn smiled. She turned to Meg. "What do you think?"

Meg nodded. "The red one, I guess."

"Why don't you take them for a test drive around the neighborhood."

Shawn laughed. "Are you sure you can trust us?"

"I think I can," Nick said. "After all, I know where both of you work, and I know where Meg lives. Just don't take too long. I close in an hour."

It appeared that Meg might nix the idea, but Shawn hurriedly said, "You've got a point. And we won't be long. Just a spin around the block. Then, if we buy them, we can think about where to go tomorrow."

Nick nodded. "Have you two thought about where you'd like to ride?"

He purposely looked at Meg, but her eyes were glued on a display of sportswear to her right. He was about to ask her what the hell he'd done to her, then decided that silence was probably his best bet considering they not only worked, but also lived, next door to each other.

"We thought we'd go to the park and ride the paths. Or the Promenade," Shawn put in when Meg didn't speak.

Nick wondered if maybe Gary could be right . . . he'd lost the legendary Morgan charm. "You might want to schedule your rides either very early in the morning, before lunch, or right after lunch, because noon and late afternoon are the times that most people get out."

Meg nodded and spared him a brief glance. "We'll do that. Thanks."

Shawn looked annoyed, but just shrugged as she wheeled her bike behind Meg toward the door. "We'll be back in about half an hour, Nick."

Nick waved as they left. "Take your time."

When the door shut, Gary laughed. "I can't believe it. The Nickster has been cut down."

Knowing exactly what Gary was referring to, Nick feigned ignorance. "What?"

"What? That girl not only gave you the cold shoulder, Nick. She gave you the cold body. Brr...I thought you were going to need a sweater."

"I don't know. I think she likes me," Nick said.

Gary just laughed. "I've heard of people suffering from delusions, Nick, but this is sad. That girl wouldn't give you a glass of water if your hair was on fire."

The hint of challenge in Gary's voice didn't go unnoticed by Nick. But at the moment, he chose to ignore it. Because beyond her aloof manner, there was something else about Meg Porter that intrigued him. And he wasn't quite sure what it was. Just that feeling of déjà vu again.

"There's something about her, Gary," he said slowly.

Gary chuckled. "And how."

Nick frowned at his friend. "Not that. Something else. Something about her voice."

"How could you tell? She hardly said anything."

Two more customers came in then, and Gary left to go home. But even as Nick helped his customers, his mind tried to figure out what it was about Meg that seemed so familiar.

"What is the matter with you, Meg?"

They were six blocks from the bike shop and had just stopped for traffic at a corner. "What do you mean?"

"You know what I mean. You just clammed up when we were at Nick's. One second you're fine and the next you become an icicle. I think Nick was really interested in you at first, but after you froze him out, he probably thinks *you* aren't interested."

Meg scowled at the Don't Walk signal. "Maybe I'm not interested. Why should you assume that I would automatically be interested in him?"

"I don't know, maybe because he's great looking and has a great body, and could string more than three words together in a halfway intelligent sentence? I just wish he'd been looking at me the way he was looking at you."

Meg looked over at her friend. "How was he looking at me?"

Shawn rolled her eyes, then looked around them. But they were alone on the corner. "Like he was a man dying of thirst and you were the last drink of water on this continent."

"Oh, he was not."

"I thought you didn't notice how he was looking at you."

Meg sighed. "All I noticed was that he seemed a lot more interested in me from the neck down than from the neck up."

"Aha!" Shawn pounced. "So you did notice."

"How could I not notice? He was talking to my chest."

The light changed and they pedaled across the street and into the neighborhood park where Shawn stopped again.

Meg knew she was going to get another of Shawn's lectures, and so resigned, stopped beside her friend.

Shawn waited until Meg looked at her. "Men are going to look, Meg, they can't help themselves. Although I don't think he was drooling. Just appreciative. I was jealous."

Meg stared at her. "You weren't."

"I was. For a couple of seconds. I would think you'd be used to it by now."

"I'll never get used to it," Meg muttered.

Shawn must have heard the hesitation in her friend's voice. "Hey, does this really bother you so much?"

Meg shook her head determinedly. "No. At least not as much as it used to. You're right. It's stupid."

"I never said it was stupid. We all have body neuroses. Mine has to do with my nose."

"What's wrong with your nose?"

Shawn laughed. "To you, nothing. To me, it's too big."

"It is not."

"Thanks. But I don't believe you, any more than you believe me. But we aren't going to let these hang-ups about body parts become a drag on our personalities, are we?"

Meg had to agree with Shawn. "I guess we shouldn't. I'll try not to let it bother me, but—"

"No buts! Just smile and pretend that every man is interested in you solely for your mind."

"I don't think I can pretend that much." Meg smiled.

"Well, do the best you can. Think about how great we'll feel after a few weeks of riding around Brooklyn on our new bikes.... I kind of like mine. Tomorrow morning we will begin our exercise regimen. Then, not only will men stare at your chest, but they'll also stare at the rest of you. Your legs, your buns—"

Meg groaned. "Just what I need."

"You and me, too," Shawn sighed. "Nice buns and maybe Nick's friend, Gary. What do you think of him?"

"He was kind of cute, I guess," Meg said. Although she had to really concentrate to remember anything specific about him. She'd been too absorbed by Nick Morgan to notice much about his friend.

"Yeah, I thought so, too," Shawn said. "Cute, in a smirky sort of way. But I can live with smirky."

Meg laughed. "Are you planning to get married anytime soon?"

"Hey, don't laugh. You never know. You have to meet the man you're going to marry sometime, somewhere. Don't you ever wonder when you meet a man, if this might be the 'one'?"

If she did, she hadn't realized it. Meg shook her head. "I guess not."

Shawn looked disappointed. "That's the trouble with you. No imagination. Come on, we'd better get back to Nick's and pay for these bikes."

Meg rolled slowly after Shawn and wondered if her friend might be right. Maybe she really didn't have any imagination.

Then she thought about Nick Morgan and frowned. If she was going to imagine herself marrying someone she'd just met, it certainly wouldn't be a man like Nick, who made it so obvious what he was thinking.

Just once, Meg thought, it would be nice to talk to a man whose eyes didn't constantly stray away from her face.

Chapter Two

Nick let himself into his apartment and tossed his helmet next to the sofa. He'd gone for a ride after he'd sold the two bikes to Meg and Shawn and closed his store. But all through his ride, something about Meg had been niggling at his brain. He'd give up, determined that he'd never figure it out, then catch himself trying another scenario.

His telephone rang just as he was popping the top on a soda and he picked up the kitchen extension.

"Hello?"

"Hey, sounds like the cold is just about whipped."

"Allison. Yeah, it's just about gone. I think drinking all of that orange juice drowned it."

His sister laughed. "Right. Not to mention the chicken soup."

"Not to mention..." He started to agree with her, then remembered what his wrong number had said. He remembered what she'd said, and he thought he remembered what she'd sounded like. Was it possible? No. Maybe?

"Nick? James Nicholas Morgan," Allison called in a singsong voice. When no response was forthcoming, she added, "Junior?"

Nick scowled at the phone. "Don't call me that."

He heard laughter coming from his sister's apartment, several blocks away. "It's not my fault you weren't listening. And it's not my fault that Dad wanted to name you after himself. It's a macho thing, I think. You'll probably end up naming your first son James Nicholas Morgan, the Third."

"No, I won't," Nick denied. "It was confusing enough growing up with someone else's name. I don't want to push the burden onto my son."

"We'll see," Allison chimed. "But anyway, I just wanted to call and make sure you hadn't died from your cold."

Nick toyed with the buttons on his telephone. "Right. I thank you for your sisterly concern."

"You're welcome. Are you coming out to the house this weekend?"

"Probably. Are you?"

"I guess. Joey likes to visit with Grandma and Grandpa."

Nick chuckled. "I would, too, if I were him. They give him presents every time they see him."

"I know. He's spoiled rotten. Well, I've gotta go and give him a bath. I'll see you this weekend."

"Right. 'Bye, Allison."

He hung up the phone and continued to gaze at the numbers. What had she said her number was? Allison's was 555-5682. The woman on the phone obviously had the same exchange as Allison, but one of the four numbers that followed was different. Was it the first number or the last? He stared at the placement of the numbers. The last, he decided. He wouldn't have messed up the first number, because it was the fourth five in a row. Now, was the last number a one or a three? Nick was pretty sure it was the three. A fifty-fifty chance, regardless.

He picked up the phone, dialed the number and waited. One ring. Two. Three.

"Hello?"

Was it she? He wasn't sure. His accent slid into place, and Nick cleared his throat.

"Hi, it's...um...it's your wrong number. Remember? From last night?"

"Oh," she said. "Sure. Your cold is better, isn't it?"

Nick smiled. It *was* she. He knew it was. "Oh, yeah, sure. I think it was the O.J. I just wanted to call and see how you were doing. You seemed sorta upset last night."

"Well, I guess I was, but it didn't last long. He just wasn't important enough to me for it to linger for very long."

"That's good. Um...listen, does it bother you that I called you again? I mean, I know that you don't know me and all, and that most women would be justified in just hanging up and calling the cops..."

She sighed. "I suppose I should hang up and change my number, but you know, I don't think I will. I don't think you're a weirdo, and I sort of liked talking with you last night."

"You did?"

"Yes. You were very straightforward about some things, and I needed that. My self-confidence isn't always what it should be, and I know that it's something I need to work on. As a matter of fact, I took your advice."

Nick frowned, and tried to think of what he'd said. "You did?"

"Yes, I'm going to start working out. Aerobics, and cycling a few days a week. I bought a secondhand bike today."

It really was Meg. Nick remembered how she appeared standing in his store as she refused to look him in the eye for more than two seconds at a time. And it wasn't just his imagination that she sounded friendlier now than she had just a few hours ago. He couldn't believe Meg Porter was the woman he'd accidentally called. And he had no idea what he should do now. Should he confess? Should he pretend he didn't know her? He had to say something, because she was waiting.

"Yeah, that's right. Working out is important. Gotta keep the blood circulating."

"Do you work out?"

"Yeah. I . . . jog, and sometimes I ride a bike, too."

"A friend and I are going to ride in a park, the traffic is too crazy for me. Um . . . do you mind if I ask you your name? I mean, just your first name. I feel like I'm talking with a stranger, but then again, I don't."

Nick hesitated. "My first name is . . . James."

"James," Meg repeated. "I'm Meg."

Despite a niggle of guilt over his minor deception, Nick couldn't help but feel a certain dash of excitement. "Meg. That's pretty. Is it short for Margaret?"

"Yes. Do your friends call you Jimmy?"

Nick closed his eyes. "Not really."

Meg laughed. "I guess you got tired of that, huh? James is more adult, more sophisticated."

"I don't think I'm sophisticated."

Meg laughed. "Neither am I. I wonder if anyone from Brooklyn can be."

"Are you from Brooklyn?"

"Yes. Well, Brooklyn Heights, actually."

"Yeah, well that's still Brooklyn. I'm from Brooklyn, too," Nick added.

"I kind of figured," Meg said.

"What do you mean?"

"Your accent."

"Oh, yeah."

"It doesn't bother you, does it?" She sounded so sincere, and he was beginning to feel guilty.

"No, not really. Usually I don't even notice. But sometimes I think maybe I should try to lose it. A . . . friend of mine did that. Went to classes and lost his accent."

"Really? Is he glad he did it?"

Nick paused. Was he happy he'd standardized his voice? "I think he is. Business types take him more seriously now. Although the accent comes right back when he's around family."

"Yeah," Meg agreed. "I never really got a Brooklyn accent, since I moved here from Virginia when I was about ten. But I had a Southern accent that I guess I've mostly lost."

"I thought your voice sounded sort of different."

Meg laughed. "Right. A sort of Southern Brooklynese."

"Ah, you sound okay to me."

"Thanks, James."

"Anytime. Listen, I gotta go. Maybe I'll call you again."

"Sure," she said. "I kind of like talking to you."

"'Bye, Meg."

"'Bye, James."

"Can I help you find something?"

The middle-aged woman looked up at Meg from the row of new fiction titles she studied. "I don't know. I'm looking for a book, but I don't know the title or the author. I think it has a blue cover, though."

Meg sighed inwardly. Not another one. Pasting a helpful expression on her face, she said, "Well, do you know what subject it is? Is it fiction?"

The woman frowned. "I'm not sure. A friend of mine saw the author on a talk show yesterday. I think it was Oprah. Or was it Donahue? Anyway, she said she wanted the book, and I wanted to get it for her for a birthday present."

Ever alert to the media promotions of books she carried via the home office of the store, Meg nodded. "Well, there was an author on Oprah yesterday. I think that the book was an autobiography."

Five minutes later the woman had purchased her blue-covered book and left the store. Shawn, standing behind the counter, next to the cash register, just shook her head.

"I think it's amazing how any of us can find anything for anybody sometimes."

Meg laughed. "We are superior puzzle-solvers and deduction artists."

"Sure. Now, on to more interesting topics...are you ready to hit the park again tomorrow morning?"

"Um...yes, I think I am."

Shawn grinned. "A little sore in the nether regions?"

They both laughed. "It's been a while since I rode a bike," Meg confessed. "But it was fun, wasn't it?"

"Except for when I almost ran over that little kid on the roller skates."

"I guess we have to watch out for things like that."

"You know," Shawn said, "you've been kind of quiet today. Is something wrong?"

Meg smiled. She wasn't sure if she wanted to talk about James to anyone, even Shawn, and she had been preoccupied with him lately. Although she didn't really know why. She was sure she'd never meet him and probably never speak with him again.

"Last night my wrong number called again."

"What? I hope you hung up on him."

"No, I didn't. I talked with him awhile."

"You what?" Shawn abruptly lowered her voice when several customers glared at her. "Are you crazy? He could be a nut, a psycho, a killer."

Meg's chin rose stubbornly. "I don't think so. He sounds perfectly normal. Besides, he can't know where I live. He didn't even know my name."

"Didn't? You didn't tell him your name?"

"Not all of it," Meg hedged. "Just my first name."

"All right, so what's his first name?"

"James," Meg smiled. "And I know it sounds unorthodox, but I like him. He's nice . . . and for some reason, I feel that I can talk to him easier than a lot of people I know. Especially men."

Shawn looked skeptical. "I still think it's weird. But, at the same time, I can understand how talking to a totally unknown person could free some inhibitions."

"Exactly," Meg enthused. "That's how I felt when I talked to him. Like I didn't have to watch what I said for fear he might think I'm stupid or gauche. Who cares? I don't even know what he looks like. And if he does start to get weird, I can just hang up and change my number."

"You know, there might be something in this. Sort of an unidentified, free counselor. You don't have to worry about what they think of you or who they might tell. You're completely anonymous."

Meg turned and picked up some special order forms from a shelf behind the counter. "I'm glad you finally understand where I'm coming from on this, Shawn. I was afraid that I might be the only one who saw it as something nonthreatening."

"Oh, I wouldn't go that far," Shawn drawled. "After all, this could all still be threatening. There's just too much you don't know about a total stranger. You'd have to watch everything you said to make sure he didn't find out where you live and work and play. And then hope he doesn't have a friend down at the phone company."

As she walked down the main aisle of the store, toward the back room and her office, Meg decided that she would

be careful on the phone, but if James called again, she knew
she'd talk with him. There was just something about the
sound of his voice that she trusted.

"Ten laps," Shawn panted as they slowed down and
pulled off the path in the park Sunday morning. "Ten laps
around this park. What is that? Ten miles?"

Meg shook her head. "I think it's more like three or
four."

Shawn groaned. "No way. Maybe we should have stuck
with aerobics."

"No. Too much aerobics is bad for your joints."

"Well, well, look who's here, Nick. So, we meet again,"
Gary called out as he and Nick pulled up behind them.

Meg didn't respond to Gary's rather predictable line.
Shawn, on the other hand, didn't waste time. "Yes, Meg
and I are trying to make cycling a part of our exercise rou-
tines. And, judging from the way we feel after only ten laps,
I would say that it was a good decision."

"It'll get easier after a while," Nick assured her. "I usually ride ten or fifteen miles a day."

Both Meg and Shawn groaned at that. Shawn blew her
bangs up off her forehead. "All by yourself? Don't you get
bored?"

Nick shook his head. "Not really. Although I do usually
take my Walkman with me."

"Well, I think it's easier to ride with a friend," Shawn
declared. "That way, you can look out for each other."

"And four friends are better than two," Gary added.
"When do you open the store on Sundays?"

"At noon," Meg said automatically.

"So do I," Nick offered. Meg already knew that but
didn't say anything.

"Well, then. Why don't we all go out for something to eat
after riding this open range?"

The suggestion came from Gary, but Nick nodded and looked at her, Meg thought uneasily. She knew she shouldn't have worn the ripped and worn sweatshirt. Its collar was gone and it was far too snug. But she hadn't expected to meet anyone she knew. Tempted though she was, Meg forced herself not to cross her arms over her chest.

Shawn laughed. "Eat back all the calories we've burned off?"

Nick shook his head. "Not that you two have anything to worry about," he smiled easily. "But we have to eat, and experts say that you burn calories faster after working out."

A quick look at his lean, taut body, and Meg wondered how Nick had come to learn such facts, when they obviously were of no use to him.

While she covertly contemplated him, Shawn and Gary made a date for all of them to meet back at the stores, then walk over to a small restaurant/deli a few blocks from there for brunch.

"Come on," she urged Meg as the men rode off down the path. "We have to shower and dry our hair and put on some makeup and get dressed."

"But they're still riding," Meg argued as Shawn got on her bike and pointed it back toward Meg's place.

"I know that," Shawn called over her shoulder. "But I have little doubt that they go faster than us, and will get back to Nick's faster than us. We'll be lucky if we're not late."

They were late, but only by a few minutes. After listening to several good-natured remarks about the time women took to get ready to go anywhere, they made their way to the restaurant, where they ordered croissants and bagels with fruit salads.

"Meg," Nick began after the waiter left, "I know you manage the bookstore, but how many other employees are there besides Shawn here?"

"Shawn is my assistant," Meg said. "There are four part-timers who work mostly nights and weekends."

"Like now?"

"Usually Shawn and I alternate Sundays, but every once in a while we work it together. I would imagine that you have quite a few employees with two stores."

"Don't get him started," Gary protested.

Shawn laughed. "Why not? I think it's great. But why did you decide on a bike shop?"

"I've always liked cycling, and worked in a shop for several years while I was in high school and college. Then I saved up enough money and bought my own place about four years ago. A few months ago I opened up the second shop."

Shawn moved her orange juice aside so the waiter could put their food on the table. "Well, I'm impressed. You're a real entrepreneur."

Gary cleared his throat loudly. "Isn't anyone interested in what I do?"

"No," Nick answered.

"My friend," Gary said, wounding himself with an imaginary dagger.

Shawn grinned at Gary. "All right, what is this fascinating job you do that we'll be monumentally impressed by?"

Frowning at Shawn, Gary shrugged. "I'm a dentist."

Meg couldn't help but laugh as Shawn clutched her mouth and groaned. Nick laughed at Gary's wounded expression.

"Sorry, pal, but dentists just aren't as impressive as bike shop owners."

Gary shook his finger at all of them. "None of you would think that if your teeth hurt. Oh, no, that's when you come running to the dentist, begging him to please help you. Please take away the pain. We are a maligned group of professionals, we are. We help, we make people look better and feel better, and what thanks do we get? None. People avoid us.''

"Oh, simmer down," Shawn sighed. "I promise I'll floss after I get home."

During the meal, Meg wasn't sure what to think about Nick. Gary was easy to figure out. He was just looking for a good time and a few laughs. At first, Meg thought that Nick was the same type. He was a jock who owned a bike shop, but he also seemed capable of carrying on an intelligent conversation about a variety of subjects. If only he'd stop looking at her with what she could only describe as bedroom eyes. It wasn't the first time she'd garnered similar looks. And they never failed to make her feel uncomfortable and self-conscious.

"Listen," Nick said as they were all getting ready to leave. "One of my distributors gave me four tickets for opening day at Shea Stadium. Why don't we all go?"

Shawn yelled, "Yes!"

Meg was about to refuse, then realized that she really would like to go, and nodded hesitantly. After receiving a strange smile of what seemed like approval from Nick, they all headed for the door, discussing the arrangements as they walked.

Several hours later Meg locked up and climbed the stairs to her tiny apartment above the bookstore. She kicked off her shoes and dropped her purse on the coffee table. Still wondering what it was about Nick Morgan that intrigued her and made her apprehensive at the same time, she pulled her clothes off and dug into the bureau next to her sofa. She found her nightgown and dropped it over her head, then wrapped herself in her warmest robe and flipped on the radio.

She plopped down in her only armchair and picked up a new bestseller that she'd borrowed from work and curled up to read. When the phone rang a few minutes later, she groped out with her right hand, her eyes still on the page where someone was about to be murdered.

"Hello?"

"Hi, Meg, it's me."

Her eyes abandoned the murder. "James! How are you?"

"I'm doing all right. You?"

His Brooklyn accent made her smile. It sounded so real, so honest, so... trustworthy. "I'm fine, James. I went out earlier with some friends, and it looks like I'm going to see the Mets on opening day."

"No kidding? I heard tickets were hard to come by."

"I suppose they are," Meg shrugged. "I didn't have to get them. My... um... friends did."

"Old friends?"

Meg frowned. "Yes and no. One old friend, two new friends. My friend Shawn and I are going with... a man who lives next door to me and his friend. One of them has the tickets."

"Oh, I get it. You gotta be careful about strange men, though."

"I know." She hesitated, then added, "As a matter of fact, Shawn warned me about you."

"Me?"

"Yes. She said that since I didn't know you, you could be a murderer or nut or something."

He laughed, the sound of his low voice tickling Meg's ear over the wire. "I suppose I could be. You just never know, do you? For that matter, these two guys you met could be nuts, too."

"Oh, they are," Meg assured him. "But not in a bad way, I don't think."

She then briefly recounted her day. "I think they can be trusted. To a point. Especially since Shawn and I are together whenever we see them."

"Oh, so it's just the gang getting together once in a while?"

Meg thought about the heated gazes she'd gotten from Nick and grew warm. "Yes, it is."

"Really?" he said after a brief pause. "You mean you don't have designs on one of these guys?"

"Of course not."

"What, of course not? They a couple of bowsers?"

Thinking of Nick's handsome face and hard, muscled body, she smiled. "Hardly."

"Oh? What's this I hear? Maybe you like one of them?"

"I don't know, James. I am attracted to one of them, but he...I don't know how to say this. I think he's only interested in me from my neck down."

A pause of several seconds lapsed over the line. "Really? You got a good body, then, Meg?"

She didn't think she should really answer that. "Let me just say that I don't like it when men stare at my...body and make it obvious that getting me into bed is more important to them than getting to know me as a person."

"Yeah, we men have one-track minds, don't we?" Then, before Meg could muster a protest, he went on. "Maybe you should give this guy a chance, Meg. Sure, maybe he likes to look, but that's not to say he wouldn't also like you as a person."

"You think so? Most of the men I've dated have been the grab-first, get-to-know-you-second types. And I don't think Nick is interested in me as a person. A body, yes, but—"

"What is this guy, a slobbering animal?"

Meg gasped. "No! Is that the impression I've given? I guess I really shouldn't say anything about him at all, since I've only just met him."

"I think you're right. Wait until you see how he acts at the ball game. And after. See how he treats you."

"You think so?"

"Oh, sure. Uh, you wouldn't freak if he tried to kiss you, would you?"

Meg frowned. "No, I wouldn't freak. I just don't like men I hardly know pawing me on a first date. Call me old-fashioned, but I like to get to know someone before letting them paw me."

"All right, I get it." James chuckled.

Meg laughed with him. She couldn't remember the last time she'd talked so openly with a man. She rarely talked this openly with her girlfriends.

"Call me next weekend, James," she said cheekily, "and I'll let you know how it went."

Nick frowned after he hung up the telephone. Now what was he supposed to do? He'd never had such a candid conversation with a woman...about himself. And, apparently, his own wandering eyes and lustful intentions.

His smile was rueful, but Nick had to admit that his eyes had wandered over Meg's luscious curves and his thoughts had—more than once—turned lustful. And he didn't feel the least bit remorseful. In fact, this wrong number thing might just prove to be his ticket past the rigid defenses of the sexy Meg Porter.

Why was he suddenly so determined to have Meg? Nick wondered as he gazed at his blank television screen. Usually if a woman wasn't interested—not a frequent happening—he let it go and went on to the next woman. But with Meg...Meg was interested, he thought confidently. She'd told James as much. She just had a few hang-ups. And for the life of him, he couldn't figure out why. She had a body most women were jealous of and most men drooled over.

"But if you don't want to be drooled over, honey, you won't be," he said to the empty room. "Nick Morgan will be the picture of gentlemanly decorum. At least for the first date or so."

* * *

On the Mets' opening day, Meg was a mass of worries. Her hair wouldn't curl right, she was sure her clothes were all wrong, and she had a pimple on her chin that she was sure was blinking like a red light despite the cover-up foundation she'd used.

She hurried to the front door when she heard the bell and barely took the time to peer through the peephole before she jerked it open.

"Shawn, am I dressed all right? How cold is it supposed to get? Should I braid my hair? I think it looks stupid."

"Geez, chill out. What's the matter with you? You act like you're going to your senior prom. It's a ball game. Who cares about your hair? The wind will destroy it anyway."

Meg grabbed her brush. "Right. So I'll braid it." As she twisted her hair into a French braid, she continued to talk to Shawn.

"Should we take blankets? It's still pretty cold out."

With a glance down at the blanket she'd dropped by the door, Shawn shrugged. "I guess. Why don't you bring an electric one and a real long extension cord?"

It took Meg a moment to realize that her friend was joking. "Very funny. Can you see this pimple?"

"What pimple?"

"The one the size of a baseball on my chin!"

Shawn leaned closer to Meg and squinted, then finally said, "Oh, yeah. Wow. Maybe you shouldn't go. Nick might be totally repulsed and refuse to let you go in with us."

"You're not taking this seriously, Shawn."

"I'm being as serious as the subject deserves. Now, come on, we have to meet the guys downstairs in five minutes. Did you know that your neighbors are really weird?"

"Nick's one of my neighbors."

"I mean the one behind you. There was some big, hairy guy who wanted to know where we were going and then told us he was a Yankees' fan and hoped the Mets lost."

Meg smiled. "That's Mr. Pellegrini. And he's not weird, just opinionated . . . and a bit nosy. I don't really mind."

Shawn nodded and looked around Meg's apartment. "Whenever I see this closet you live in, I'm glad I still live at home with my parents."

Gathering up an old blanket, Meg stuffed it into a canvas bag with a thermos of hot chocolate. "That would be a little inconvenient for me, since my parents now live in Sarasota."

Down the flight of slightly rickety wooden steps they went, Shawn complaining about them nearly all the way. Once outside, they saw a dark brown convertible, its top up, pulling up to the curb.

Gary and Nick jumped out and waved.

"Ready?"

Meg smiled weakly at Nick, and thought about the advice James had given her almost a week before. She'd tried to do as James had suggested all week, every time she'd seen Nick. And so far, he hadn't done anything more suggestive than offer to sweep her sidewalk. And stranger still, she hadn't caught him leering at her once in the past week.

But that had been just a few minutes here and there. This was a social outing lasting most of the day. Just see how he treats me, she thought. She glanced back at him after greeting Gary, and Meg was startled to realize that Nick was looking directly into her eyes. And his gaze didn't falter or wander. He just smiled. And Meg's pulse jumped into overdrive.

"I'm as ready as I'll ever be," she mumbled as she let him take her bag and put it in the trunk.

The day was slightly overcast, the sun trying, without much success, to break through the clouds. The four baseball fans all wore blue jeans and sweatshirts or sweaters. Meg and Shawn had turtleneck shirts on underneath sweatshirts emblazoned with cartoon characters. Nick wore a multi-colored crew neck sweater, and Gary, an N.Y.U. sweatshirt.

"Good thing we all brought blankets," Gary said as he slammed the trunk shut. "Because it could get mighty cool before the game's over."

He and Shawn got into the front seat and Nick and Meg into the back.

"Nice car," Shawn said as they started toward the stadium. "I like convertibles."

"Maybe we can go for some rides in the country this summer," Gary suggested.

"I prefer riding my bike in the summer," Nick said.

Meg smiled at him, and forced herself to speak normally. "You know what I've always thought would be interesting? Going on one of those long biking trips. You know, when you cycle and camp and hike and swim and everything for a week. We used to go camping when I was a kid, but I've never done the cycling part. I saw a TV special on some people who cycled through the mountains. Have you ever done that?"

Nick nodded. "Every summer. I go up to the Catskills or the Adirondacks. Vermont and New Hampshire are also great."

"No way," Shawn stated from the front seat. "Sleeping with a lot of bugs and wearing myself out on a bike all day long is not my idea of a vacation. I want to go on a cruise and be waited on hand and foot."

"Ah, a woman after my own heart," Gary sighed. "I never could understand the attractions of insects, chapped lips and sore behinds. Give me a deck chair and a cool drink and I'll be happy."

The rest of the trip to Shea Stadium was spent reviewing various vacations they'd all had and ones they'd like to take if they had the time and money. By the time they'd found a parking place and managed to actually get inside the stadium, Meg realized that she'd forgotten to be nervous around Nick. He'd been so casual and generally friendly that she'd relaxed more easily than she'd thought possible. Maybe he wasn't after her body after all, she thought. Maybe he just wants to be friends now.

Why did that thought distress her more than thinking he was a lech?

"Meg? Is something wrong?"

She looked into Nick's concerned hazel eyes and felt a fluttering in her stomach. He really was so much better looking than any man she'd ever gone out with. "No, nothing's wrong," she said, and smiled, dropping her gaze as she heard Shawn and Gary calling to them.

The game passed rather uneventfully, with the Mets winning, to their hometown crowd's delight. By the fifth inning, Meg and Shawn had wrapped themselves in their blankets, and by the seventh, were sharing them with Nick and Gary. Meg knew it should have been the perfect time for Nick to make a pass, but he didn't. He was polite and considerate. He probably isn't interested in me anymore, she thought dispiritedly as they made their way back to the car. I just imagined he was. Or if he was, I squashed it by not encouraging him.

Not much was said that didn't pertain to the game on the way back to Meg's apartment. Once there, Gary offered to give Shawn a ride back to her place, and they waved goodbye to Nick and Meg as they stood in the doorway that led to Meg's apartment. A moment of awkward silence ensued after Gary and Shawn drove away. Then Meg turned and opened her downstairs door and started up the stairs. Nick followed.

All the way up the wooden flight of stairs, Meg tried desperately to think of something interesting or clever to say but couldn't come up with a thing. She hadn't asked him to come up, but then she noticed that he was carrying her bag and figured he was just being polite. Then he followed her in when she opened the door to her apartment.

Nick set the bag down and looked around her apartment. "This reminds me of an apartment in an old movie I saw once. Only there were two people living in it and they couldn't turn around in it without bumping into each other."

Meg laughed. "It was probably filmed here. I manage to turn around without injuring myself too severely, but then, I live alone."

"I'm glad my store came with that apartment above it. It's saving me a lot of money."

"I imagine so," Meg said. "The company that owns the bookstore lets me have this place for practically nothing...which is all it's worth. I can't really complain, because I'm saving all my money so that I can buy my parents' old house. Can I get you something to drink? Beer? Soda?"

"What kind of beer?"

"Light."

"All right."

She knew Nick watched her as she moved about in her small kitchen and Meg found it hard to perform even the simplest of motions gracefully. She handed him his beer, then took her own and sat down on the sofa. Nick sat at the other end, but on her sofa, that still wasn't very far away.

"What was that about buying your parents' house? Are they moving?"

Meg shook her head. "No, they already moved. To Florida. They were going to sell their house, but decided to rent it instead, until I could save up enough for a down payment. They wanted to give it to me, but I know they couldn't afford that. They live on a fixed income now and need the money. Besides, they're willing to sell it to me for a ridiculously low price, considering where it is.''

Nick sipped his beer and nodded. "And where is it?"

"About eight blocks from here, on a very pretty, quiet, tree-lined street."

"Sounds great. How long do you think it will take you to save the money?"

Meg grimaced. "At the rate I'm going, about five years."

Nick didn't say anything then, he just hummed and sipped his beer. Meg did the same, and wondered why she couldn't just talk with him easily, as she had earlier. For that matter, why couldn't she talk with Nick as easily as she talked with James on the phone?

Because James was a stranger and didn't touch her life in a tangible, physical way, she thought. Nick did. Being around Nick made her heart beat faster and her skin tingle. Apparently her tongue numbed around him, as well, because she couldn't seem to say anything intelligible, much less intelligent.

He set his empty beer bottle on the coffee table and Meg looked at him tentatively. "Would...would you like another?"

Nick shook his head. "No, thanks. Meg? Is something wrong?"

"Wrong? No, nothing's wrong. Why do you ask?"

"I don't know. You seem sort of quiet. Would you rather I left?"

"No!" Meg hadn't meant to sound quite so desperate. "No, of course not. Unless, of course, you want to leave."

"No," he said.

"Um, would you like to listen to some music?" Meg suggested with a gesture at her small stereo unit. "I have rather eclectic taste in music, so you should find something you like."

"Okay," he said, and rose to step over to the stereo. Meg also rose, intending to take the empty beer bottles to the kitchen. Due to the cramped confines of her apartment, however, she had to get around Nick to get to the kitchen.

"Excuse me," she said, her voice a little too breathless, considering she hadn't done any marathon running lately.

"Oh, sure," he said as he turned sideways. Meg tried to slide past him without touching him, but certain parts of her body were just incapable of being sucked in.

The brush of her breasts against his chest sent waves of sensual awareness zinging along her skin, down into her stomach and back up through her chest. She blinked in amazement at her body's reaction, and looked up at Nick, who gazed down into her face with blatant desire hovering in his eyes. Meg swallowed heavily and looked away. She didn't want him to see the relief in her eyes. Nick wanted them to be more than just friends after all.

"I'll . . . I'll be right back."

But before she could move past him, Nick had wrapped one hand around her waist, stopping her. "No, wait."

She looked up carefully, almost afraid of what she might see. She was about to ask what he wanted when the descent of his head made it perfectly clear what he wanted.

The first touch of his lips on hers almost made Meg drop the two beer bottles she was holding. It was as if he knew how important this kiss was to her, she thought as his lips lightly tasted hers, then drew back, then settled more firmly to coax a response that had waited just for him to awaken it.

Not being able to touch him, all her senses were concentrated right on that kiss, and to Meg, it made it all the more intense. And it was a kiss like no other she'd ever experienced. When Nick finally pulled away and looked at her, his eyes were hooded and filled with a sexual awareness that she felt right down to her toes.

"Mmm" was the only response Meg could manage.

Nick just smiled.

Chapter Three

Meg blinked her eyes open slowly and stared hazily at Nick's pleased smile. She wondered what he was thinking, then thought that it was probably better that she didn't know.

She cleared her throat shakily and waved her arms up and down, trying to bring attention to the two beer bottles still clutched in her now sweaty hands. Nick released the hold he had on her waist, and Meg continued across the room to the kitchen, where she placed the bottles on the counter and then leaned against it, trying to gather her scattered thoughts.

Just as she thought she'd done so, she felt Nick's arms encircle her waist from behind, and her thoughts scattered again.

He nuzzled her neck with warm, moist lips for a moment, mumbling incoherent words that sounded terribly sexy to Meg. Her breath caught each time his lips touched

her skin, and when he turned her in his arms, she was afraid
she might hyperventilate.

"I've been wanting to kiss you like that ever since I met
you," he said softly.

"You have?"

"Yes. And guess what?"

Meg trembled slightly at the raspy quality of his voice.
"What?"

"I don't think I can stop at just one."

Then he kissed her again, and Meg just leaned into him,
returning his kisses, as well as his caresses, since her hands
were now free to roam across his wide shoulders and up into
his thick hair and down over the muscles of his arms...
There was a solid strength in Nick's body that made her feel
more feminine than she ever had. But there was also a powerful need building in her that she knew she'd never felt for
any other man. She almost told him, but then decided
against any confessions at this point.

Honesty was admirable, she thought fuzzily as Nick's
teeth nipped at her earlobe, but as much as she wanted to tell
Nick what she was feeling, Meg was more afraid of appear-
ing gauche and inexperienced. Would Nick laugh if she expressed her romantic feelings? Maybe not, but Meg wasn't
yet willing to lay her feelings on the line like that. She also
knew it wasn't fair to let him think more might happen than
a few kisses, so she put her hands on his chest and gently
pushed.

"What is it?" Nick mumbled, his lips on her neck.

Meg cleared her throat again and shook her head.
"Nothing's the matter. I just think that we're going a little
too fast for me. I like you, Nick, but ... I don't really know
you that well."

Nick smiled at her words, and brushed his thumbs over
the faint tinge of dark pink that touched her cheeks. "Too
fast?" He pulled his hands from her face and stepped away.

"Okay, but I can't promise it won't happen again. You might have to fight me off. I hope this isn't going to be a problem."

He was teasing her, but it was a nice sort of teasing, Meg decided. "I don't think it will be a problem," she said, afraid her smile revealed too much of her relief. She wanted desperately to appear sophisticated and cool about the situation but knew that that was impossible. Whenever she was alone with Nick, her lungs seemed to constrict and her stomach parachuted to her knees. To Meg, it was amazing that she remained as calm as she did.

Nick smiled and leaned forward to drop a sweet, brief kiss on her lips. Then he turned his attention to the albums. Meg, still feeling the heated imprint of his hard body pressed against hers, retreated to the kitchen in search of something to do with her hands. She put the beer bottles in her recycling bin, which took about five seconds. She went back into the living room as Nick dropped the needle on an album on the turntable.

For the next hour Meg was able to relax enough to enjoy listening to music and talking about various bands. Nick left after giving Meg a brief but searing kiss at her door. She felt at odds but wasn't sure what do about it, so she wandered around her small apartment, straightening things that were already straight. Spotting the album they'd listened to, she slipped it into its jacket and then held it close to her chest.

The intensity of her feelings for Nick frightened her even as they exhilarated her. Was this the beginning of something wonderful, or the prelude to the groping session their next date might bring? Meg wished she had the nerve to tell Nick exactly what she felt and why. But it was too soon.

"Besides," she said to herself, "I'd be too embarrassed. And I'm not even sure that there'll be a next date."

Nick hadn't asked her out again. Meg's face crumpled in chagrin. Maybe he was just being nice to her when he really wasn't moved by her rather inexperienced kisses. If he were interested, wouldn't he have asked her out again?

Meg shook her head and put the album away. Life was certainly an unpredictable series of discoveries, she thought as she finished cleaning up her apartment. Just a few weeks ago her life had seemed ordinary to the point of dullness. Now, every day had the prospect for adventure and excitement, and depression and self-doubt.

Trying to call Shawn proved fruitless. She wasn't home. Meg sat on her sofa and contemplated the telephone. She could call her parents but rejected the idea almost as soon as she thought of it. Her feelings for Nick weren't something she wanted to discuss with her mother. At least not yet. Maybe James would call, she thought.

"I really should get James's number," she murmured to herself.

Next door, Nick entered his apartment and tossed his things into his hall closet. Whistling, he looked at the mail he'd picked up from his box and then tossed it on his kitchen table.

Not surprisingly, he found his thoughts returning to Meg. It had been a long day and a more than interesting evening. He thought about the way Meg had responded when he'd kissed her. He'd never felt such honesty from a woman's kiss, or such a desire to put her feelings before his own. That last thought gave him pause. What was it about Meg that made him want to look out for her, protect her, even from himself? And what did she really think about him? Did she feel the same explosive desire that he did. Did she wonder about the possibility of a future between them?

His eyes were drawn to the phone, and he glared at it.

"No, I'm not going to do that anymore. It doesn't seem fair, somehow. Like I'm cheating."

But if you don't, you might never find out how she really feels, he told himself. So far, Meg hadn't exactly been a fount of information about herself. Nick hadn't asked her out again immediately, because he reminded himself that she didn't want to be rushed. But he did at least want to know if maybe she'd like to go out with him. If the kisses they'd shared were any indication, she should be willing to go with him to the Bahamas for the weekend.

Was his curiosity greater than his sense of fairness? Nick didn't think it was until he found himself dialing her number and slipping into his Brooklyn accent when he heard her say hello.

"Uh, hi, it's me," he said, wondering if he should just confess right here and now.

"James! I was just thinking about you a little while ago. I think I would have called you if I'd had your number."

Nick panicked for a few seconds. He couldn't give Meg James's phone number because Meg might ask for *Nick's* phone number.

"Oh, well, it wouldn't have done any good, since I just got home. How was the game?"

If he could distract her, maybe she wouldn't pursue the matter.

"Oh, it was great," she enthused, telling him about the game and how the Mets won.

"Sounds like a great time," he said carefully.

"It was, James, it really was. And I have to tell you that your advice was wonderful. I tried not to read motives into Nick's actions, and you know what? He was a perfect gentleman all day. In fact, for a while, I thought maybe he wasn't interested in me . . . you know, that way. . . ."

Nick was about to ask her if she was crazy, but caught himself. "That's too bad," he muttered.

"No, not really," she said quickly. "I...um...that is, he did kiss me after all, James. Despite what I thought, he kissed me. Three times."

Nick paused. "Well, good. I mean, I guess that's good."

"Oh, it was good, all right," Meg breathed through the receiver at him. "It was more than just good, it was great. I know I probably shouldn't be talking about this to you, since I don't really even know you, but I have to talk to someone, and you know, James, I really feel that you understand."

"I'm glad," he said. "And I don't think we're really strangers. We just haven't actually met."

"That's right," Meg agreed. "And I think that's what makes our conversations so easy. I think if we ever did actually meet, that it might ruin everything, don't you?"

Nick closed his eyes and rubbed them with tense fingers. "I guess so."

"Anyway, this guy is so great that I wonder if he's really like this all the time or if he's just being considerate of my feelings to lure me into a false sense of security."

"What? I mean, do you really think he'd do that?" Nick was almost afraid of hearing her answer.

"I don't know, James. I don't like to think that, but maybe I've become too skeptical. Anything could happen, you know. Nick could be secretly married, or a drug addict or a pathological liar."

Wincing at the last choice, Nick nevertheless laughed. "Sounds like this guy could be real trouble."

"Oh, you know what I mean. It's really hard to justify liking someone so much when you've only known them such a short amount of time. My dad always says that if something looks too good to be true, it probably is."

"You think this Nick guy is too good to be true?"

Meg paused. "In a way, I guess I do. He makes me feel like...like I'm beautiful and special and...and desirable. No one else has ever made me feel those things."

Nick had to cough to loosen the thickness in his throat. "Sounds like you like him and he likes you. What's your problem?"

Meg sighed. "I don't know. There's so much I want to tell him. So much about him that I wonder about. But I don't know what to say or if it's too soon. I guess I'm afraid that if I reveal too much too soon, I'll scare him off."

Nick closed his eyes. "Um, does he seem like the kind of guy who might scare easy?"

She didn't answer immediately. After a moment she said, "I don't know. I don't think so, but my judgment is suspect, you know. I have a hard time figuring men out."

"Like women are easy for men to figure out?"

Meg laughed. "I guess you're right. Maybe everyone is confused by the opposite sex. I suppose I'm just a worry-wort, always expecting something to rain on my parade."

"Into every life that rain's gotta fall," Nick intoned. "Just remember to carry your umbrella and you'll be all right."

"James, you're a philosopher as well as a psychologist."

"Yeah, right," he murmured. "Listen, I gotta go. I just wanted to call and see how everything went."

"I'm glad you did," she answered. "Things ended up going better than I thought they would, even though I tried to screw them up."

"Naw. Give yourself some credit."

"I'll try. It was great talking with you, James."

"Yeah. I'll call you again next week, maybe."

"I'd like that."

"Gary, I need to talk with you about something," Nick said quietly as they stood in Nick's store. He'd just turned the sign to Closed. He didn't have much time, because Meg and Shawn were joining them later at what was rapidly becoming a regular hangout.

"What? This doesn't have to do with one of your stores, does it?"

"No, no, it's sort of... more personal. And it's confidential. You can't tell anyone."

"Hey, no problem. It's me, Gary, your best friend since junior high school. What's the problem?"

"I'm doing something that isn't exactly honest, but that isn't illegal, but that I'm not sure how to stop."

With those enigmatic words, Nick began his explanation of his problem. When he was done, Gary just gaped at him.

"That is wild. And it started with a wrong number?"

"Yes. But now, the problem is that I know I shouldn't be calling her and talking with her, but I can't seem to stop. She opens up more and tells James more than she's willing to tell me."

"But you *are* James. Whoa, wait a minute. Why would you want to stop? How many men get the opportunity to find out what a woman really thinks about them? This is a golden chance. I'd hang onto it, if I were you."

Nick shook his head. "But don't you get it? I want to see her more, and while it seemed fun at first, it's beginning to seem like an invasion of privacy. Besides, what if she starts saying things I don't want to hear?"

"Better than not to hear them at all, or hear them when it's too late. I think you should just keep your trap shut and keep going out with her and calling her as James. If it really starts to interfere with your relationship—provided you want one with her—then just stop calling her."

Nick thought that was easier said than done, since he'd tried to make himself not call her several times, only to be overwhelmed with the desire to talk with her and hear her secrets. Because James was the only one she'd tell them to.

Meg had told him that just the other night. Or rather, she'd told James.

And, if he wanted to be honest, it bothered him that she would tell a guy she'd never met things of such a personal nature, but she wouldn't tell the guy she was going out with. The fact that they were the same man wasn't the point.

It had been several weeks since the day of the ball game, and Meg spent half her time wondering if she'd met Mr. Right and the other half waiting for the other shoe to drop.

They'd gone out on several dates, some with Gary and Shawn, some on their own. At the end of each of them, Nick had kissed her, sometimes quite senseless, but he'd never pressed her to go to bed with him. To Meg, that seemed a little strange. She wanted to be glad that he respected her, but she also wanted him to want her.

"Will you stop looking so moony and pay attention?"

Her reverie was snapped by Shawn's amused words, and Meg gave her an unapologetic shrug as she looked around the restaurant where they waited for Nick and Gary. "I was thinking about Nick."

Shawn pulled an exaggerated expression of shock. "No! Really? As if you've thought about anything or anyone else for the past few weeks. Are you guys getting serious about each other, or is this doofy expression of yours just temporary?"

"I don't know," Meg sighed. "I think I want to get more serious, but I don't know how Nick feels."

"Why don't you just ask him how he feels?"

Shawn gestured for a waiter and got a wave of acknowledgment in return. From Meg, she only got a shrug.

"I don't know. Maybe I'm afraid he's not as serious about me as I am about him."

"I don't get it," Shawn said. "You won't talk to Nick about how you feel about him, but you'll talk with this wrong number guy. I think you should hang up the telephone and focus all that attention on Nick.''

Meg squirmed in her seat. Her conversations with James had become something of a touchy situation between her and Shawn. In the past couple of weeks, she'd just about stopped telling her friend and co-worker when she'd talked with him.

"I know you don't understand why I continue to talk with James,'' Meg tried to explain. "But after I talk to him I feel better about myself. I feel more confident and I end up relating to Nick better.''

Shawn sighed. "Yes, but does Nick know you're telling a strange man details of your love life?''

"Uh, no. I didn't think that he'd really understand. Besides, James and I talk about more than just my love life. We talk about politics and books and sports and all sorts of things. I've even told him how hard it was growing up and how glad I was to graduate from high school and get away from the immature boys who cracked stupid jokes and the—''

"Wait a minute,'' Shawn interrupted. "You've discussed those kinds of really private things with this guy? You haven't even told me all of these things, have you?''

Meg blinked at her. "I guess I haven't. I'm not usually very comfortable talking about it. But James is different.''

"Maybe you should be going out with James instead of Nick,'' Shawn suggested in exasperation.

"Don't be ridiculous,'' Meg scoffed. "I could never tell a guy I was going out with the sorts of things I tell James.''

Shawn stared. "What do you mean? Don't you trust Nick enough by now to—'' But it was then that the door to the diner opened and Nick and Gary breezed in. Meg gave Shawn a warning look and leaned forward.

"We'll discuss it later.''

Shawn just shrugged and turned to greet the two men. "Hi, guys. We were just talking about you, and how interesting it is that since we met, it's taken you two longer and longer to get ready and get over here."

Gary laughed. "That's because we're trying to make ourselves as beautiful as possible for you," he simpered, until Nick slapped him in the stomach and told him to shut up and sit down. He did, but only for a few seconds.

"Announcement, announcement," Gary proclaimed, causing Shawn to shush him. "But it's important," he insisted. "No, it's monumental. You all know, of course, that it is June, and that in June there are certain things that take precedence."

Shawn sighed wistfully. "Weddings, summer vacations..."

"Baseball," Gary insisted. "Or, to be more accurate, softball."

The waiter came and took their orders, and Meg looked back at Gary. "What about softball?"

"Nick and I happen to belong to an exceptional softball league that is going coed this year, due to scores of protestations by women who were clamoring to get close to us many macho men."

"Actually," Nick laughed, "it's going coed because there aren't enough men to fill the teams anymore."

"That's right," Gary said, waving his hand in the air. "Dispel the illusion I've worked so hard to create."

The two women looked at each other. Meg frowned. Shawn smiled. "I like softball, but I think Meg is less than comfortable with team sports."

Nick leaned over the table and looked at Meg. "Is that true?"

She nodded. "I just never did very well in school at that sort of thing," she said softly. Having a dozen boys stop whatever they were doing in a gym class just to watch you run for a fly ball was not likely to induce one to pursue the game later, she thought. But she couldn't tell Nick that. James maybe, but not Nick. Not yet, anyway.

"Well, you wouldn't have to play unless you wanted to," Nick said. "But you probably will. Our team isn't exactly on the cutting edge as far as competitive spirit goes."

"I beg your pardon, you traitor," Gary retorted as he dove into his food. "We are very competitive. I, for instance, have the best shoes. Nick here has the best hair."

Meg slid her gaze over to Shawn, and then over to Nick. "The best hair?"

"It's stupid."

Gary, of course, took exception. "It most certainly is not. Take pride in your accomplishments, Nick." Then he turned to the women. "He has the best hair because no matter how hard he plays or how dirty and sweaty he gets, his hair still manages to look great. Many people have commented on this phenomenon, not just myself."

"Now we *have* to go," Shawn insisted. "This team sounds like the kind of team that I'd fit right into."

They all looked expectantly at Meg, who sighed. "All right. I'll go. But I don't know if I'll actually play."

After an encouraging conversation with James, Meg decided that she'd at least try playing softball again. Dressed in khaki walking shorts and an oversize T-shirt, with slightly ratty sneakers on her feet, Meg greeted Shawn outside the store.

"Geez, do you think you're camouflaged enough?" Shawn asked with a shake of her head.

"What?"

Shawn sighed and shrugged. "Never mind. Come on, I've got an extra glove in my bag for you. The guys left over an hour ago, because they had to go and pick up some of the other players."

Following behind Shawn, Meg noticed that her friend was dressed in short cutoffs and a tank top. Meg wouldn't have worn a similar outfit in a million years. Too many leering eyes and smarmy smirks. The last thing she wanted to do was draw attention to her body. It drew enough attention without her help.

The park where Nick and Gary's team played was the same park where Meg and Shawn cycled. They rode their bikes over, then parked and locked them to a bike stand near the baseball fields.

Locating the team wasn't very difficult, as they were the loudest, most raucous group of people present. The two women stood behind the batter's cage for a few minutes watching the team warm up.

There were many boasts and brags, and several ribald remarks, but it seemed to Meg that they were a harmless bunch, if excessive in their frolics.

Most of the men—and there were only men present—were wearing what appeared to be uniform shirts of some kind. Trying to make out the writing on the front was proving to be a fruitless endeavor for Meg when she heard Shawn's confused voice.

"What does 'Splerb Veeblie' mean?"

Meg shook her head. "I have no idea. I thought I was reading it wrong."

It was then that Nick and Gary, who'd been playing second base and shortstop, saw them and trotted over to a chorus of "women, women, women" being chanted by their teammates.

"Hey, we thought you two might have decided not to come after all," Gary smiled.

"No," Shawn denied. "We had to open the store for the part-timers, but we wouldn't have missed it. Would we, Meg?"

Meg was staring at the nonsensical words on Nick's chest, trying to find some meaning in them. "No, we wouldn't. What does that mean?"

Nick looked down to where her finger pointed at his shirt. Then he laughed and looked over at Gary, who was studying his fingernails. "Funny you should ask. Actually, I have no idea what it means. Gary is the only one who knows, and he won't tell anyone."

They all looked expectantly at Gary, who opened his mouth, then shut it and shrugged. Shawn looked from Gary back to Nick and frowned. "What's going on? What does 'Splerb Veeblie' mean?"

"Go on, Gary, tell them what it means," Nick laughed.

Gary sighed and grinned sheepishly. "I have no idea."

Thoroughly confused, Meg looked back to Nick. "Okay. Now would one of you two like to let us in on the little joke?"

After a brief glance at Gary, who just shrugged again, Nick nodded. "All right, but you have to realize that this is a team secret, not to be divulged to anyone...especially not to our competition. Their confusion is one of our weapons."

"One of our few weapons," Gary interjected.

"A few years ago, when we were putting this team together, several of us got together and we tried to come up with some ideas for a team name. Nothing was working, but it was Gary here, dentist extraordinaire, who came up with the winner. It should be noted that he'd had a few too many beers. We got up to leave when he suddenly pointed at us and said, 'Splerb Veeblie.' He doesn't remember ever saying it, and coincidentally, hasn't had a drink since."

Meg nodded, her face pensive. Shawn guffawed. Gary looked wounded.

"Of course, you have only the word of some definitely questionable characters that I ever said that."

Nick grinned at him. "That's right. But there were five of us and one of you. And we all remember the incident, which is more than you can say."

"Hey, are you guys playing, or what?"

Several raggedy-looking members of the Splerb Veeblies stood near home plate with several neat-looking members of the competition—the E Street Maulers.

"You're both playing today, aren't you?"

Nick asked them both, but directed the question mainly at Meg, who hesitated only momentarily before nodding. Gary and Shawn preceded them over to where the other players stood. An umpire was warning them all not to do any fighting or he'd go home. Meg swallowed and glanced nervously at Nick, who smiled.

The umpire then yelled for them to play ball, and Meg found herself swept over to the Veeblie bench, where various players picked up bats and swung them back and forth.

"What position can you play?"

Meg shoved her hands into the pockets of her shorts and peered up at Nick. "Um, I don't know. I haven't played since the eleventh grade. I doubt that I'd be much good anywhere."

She expected a look of long-suffering male annoyance, but she didn't see it. Nick just nodded and smiled. "I guess we'll put you in center field, then. Whoever's playing left and right fields can help you if you need it. Do you have a glove?"

Meg nodded cautiously and wondered if she'd be able to get through this whole thing. They sat down on the bench and Shawn tossed the glove she'd brought at Meg, who dropped it.

Sure she would hear snickers or groans, she quickly picked up the glove and stole a peek at Nick, but he was watching the batter approach the plate and calling encouragement to him.

The first two batters struck out and Meg began to relax a little. It appeared that the Splerb Veeblies weren't a very good team. Maybe she could come through this ordeal without feeling too embarrassed.

Gary batted third and reached first on an error. Then Nick smacked a home run that had one of the Maulers looking through the parking lot for the ball. The next batter popped up and made the third out, which emptied the Veeblie bench as they all headed for their positions on the field. Meg took her glove and put it on, flexing her fingers inside the unfamiliar leather sheath.

"Don't worry about it," Shawn said, walking with her onto the field. "It's a game, you know. The point is to have fun."

Meg tried to smile. "I know. I'm trying."

"I know you are, and you will have fun, if you'll just let yourself."

They were still in the infield when they heard a low whistle and several catcalls. Meg immediately tensed and purposely kept her eyes cast steadily straight ahead. Shawn twisted her head and waved at the Mauler bench.

"See, not everyone is staring at your chest. Some of them are staring at our behinds. I like to think at mine, in particular, since you insisted on wearing dull shorts."

Meg grinned wryly as she looked down at her decidedly frumpy attire. "I guess I did overdo it, didn't I?"

"Yes, but as long as you're comfortable, I suppose it's all right."

Meg basically stood in center field for the next five innings. Shawn was in left field and someone named Russ was in right field, although from what Meg could tell, he was mainly eating peanuts and getting a tan. The occasional fly ball was caught by one of them, without much effort.

She'd also struck out both times she'd been at bat, but no one had derided her. In fact, it was just the opposite. The other players had been very encouraging of both Meg and Shawn.

The score was tied at the bottom of the sixth, and Meg hoped she wouldn't have to bat again, since they only played seven innings, but that hope faded as the first two batters got on base. The next two batters struck out. Then Nick was handing her a bat.

"Come on, slugger, slap the lacings off that ball."

Meg took the bat and sighed. "If they come off, it will be from shock because I managed to hit it."

Nick clapped his hands and led the encouragement from the Veeblie bench. Meg thought it was inordinately sweet of all of them, especially considering how inept she was.

The first two pitches were too high and Meg didn't even bother to swing at them. Hoping she would just get a walk, she let the next one sail by. The umpire yelled "Strike!" so loudly that Meg jumped and tightened her grip on the bat, which Nick had told her to choke up on. Meg had choked up, but the two inches of bat that showed below her left fist wasn't the only choking she was doing.

The third pitch wasn't very good, but Meg swung anyway, and missed. Typical, she thought. Then, staring at the pitcher, she decided to just swing at the next pitch and get her last strikeout so that the teams could get on with playing.

Watching as the softball left the pitcher's hand, Meg waited until it was reasonably near the plate and then closed her eyes, swinging the bat out across the plate. The pressure of the ball hitting her bat startled her eyes open.

"Run, Meg!" Nick shouted from the sideline.

Meg ran.

She didn't know who'd been more surprised by the fact that she actually hit the ball: herself, the pitcher, Nick, or the second baseman, who let the ball roll by him into right field. Meg was standing on second base and the two other Veeblies had scored before the ball was recovered.

The Veeblie bench was ecstatic. At least, Meg thought they were ecstatic. From second base, they appeared thrilled. They may have just been laughing at the shocked second baseman.

The next batter was Shawn, and she managed to bunt the ball halfway between the pitcher and the third baseman. Meg didn't need to be told to run this time. She made it to third safely, and Shawn made it to first. Waving across the diamond at Meg, Shawn laughed and yelled a strange sort of whoop that the Veeblies on the bench then echoed with much volume.

Back at the top of the order, Russ was at bat, and Meg watched as he calmly ate peanuts between pitches.

"Come on, Russ," she called encouragingly, following Shawn's lead. Russ ran out of peanuts, then swung at the next pitch and smacked the ball right over Meg's head into left field. If she hadn't been stooped over, her hands on her knees, it would have hit her.

"Run," Shawn yelled, rounding second.

Meg trotted ahead of her across home plate. Shawn scored behind her, and they turned to see where Russ had ended up. To their amazement, Russ was sitting on second base, examining his knee, which had apparently been scraped as he slid into second.

Upon their triumphant return to the bench, Meg was wrapped in a bear hug by Nick and kissed loudly as Gary and Shawn went through an intricate and elaborate hand and hip slapping routine.

"No fair kissing the center fielder unless we all get to," complained several cheeky Veeblies.

"Buzz off," Nick tossed over his shoulder. To Meg, he just smiled. "See? I knew you could do it."

Meg still barely believed that she had actually done it. "I'm glad you knew, because I sure didn't. I guess I was just unsure, since I haven't played in so long, and you guys didn't have a practice game before making me play...."

"Practice?" Nick hooted. "This bunch of derelicts? Practicing isn't fun. Playing is fun. Win or lose. It's the playing that's fun. That's why we play together on our strange team. Because we want to have some fun. Are you having any?"

Meg laughed. "Yeah, I think I am."

The rest of the bench groaned then as the next batter popped out. Russ still sat on second base, and Meg carried his glove out to him and held out her hand to help him up.

She even fielded a ball that day, if running over to a ball that had stopped rolling and managing to throw it to second base could be called fielding.

The inning ended soon after that with the victorious Splerb Veeblies giving a raucous, and rather lewd, cheer for the losing team, who responded by waving assorted fingers and fists at them.

"And the Splerb Veeblies triumph once again," Gary boasted as he stood on the bench, surrounded by laughing teammates.

"Again? This is the first game we've won," the pitcher said wryly.

Meg blinked up at Nick. "You guys haven't won a single game?"

"We have now," he corrected. "Besides, this is only our fourth game of the summer. We have ten more to go. I hope you're going to play with us for the rest of the summer."

Thinking about how apprehensive she had been and then about how well things had turned out, Meg smiled up at him. "Why not? I doubt that I could really be a detriment to the team," she added, and looked over to where Russ sat on the bench, eating another bag of peanuts while he stared forlornly at his scraped knee.

Nick laughed. "No, you could never be a detriment to *this* team."

Chapter Four

Meg hummed to herself as she got ready for bed that night. She'd never thought it would be possible that she would enjoy an afternoon of softball so much. Of course, since she'd met Nick, she was beginning to believe that anything was possible. Even love.

"Am I falling in love?" she asked herself as she changed into her nightgown. How did a person know when they were in love? "All I know," Meg told her reflection as she brushed her hair, "is that I've never felt so deliciously wonderful about a man in my entire life."

She flopped down onto the bed with her spare pillow hugged to her chest and contemplated calling her mother. Or was it still too soon to tell anyone? Nick still hadn't said anything to indicate that he wanted their relationship to become more serious.

Then again, she sighed, if his heated kisses were anything to judge by, he cared more than a little for her. He continued to ask her out and treated her better than any man ever had.

The telephone on the bedside table next to her head rang and Meg turned over and pulled the receiver to her ear.

"Hello?"

"How are you doing?"

"James! How wonderful to hear from you. You're such an unpredictable guy, you know. Sometimes you don't call for weeks and other times it's two or three times in one week."

"Yeah, I know. I get busy sometimes...you know how it is. Then other times, I just think about you and call."

Meg smiled and slid down farther on her bed. "That's so sweet. I think about you sometimes, too. You really should give me your phone number, so that I don't have to wonder if you're ever going to call me again."

After a brief pause, she heard him clear his throat. "I was going to do just that, but I, uh..."

A sudden thought made Meg grit her teeth and squeeze her eyes shut with self-censure. "I'm sorry, James, I didn't even think. Are you married?"

"Married?"

From the tone of his voice, Meg felt that she'd hit the nail on the head. "I feel so stupid."

"No, don't. I'm not married."

Why was she relieved? "You aren't? You have a girl-friend, though?"

"Yeah," he said after a moment. "I hope you under-stand."

Meg laughed. "I do. And it's okay, really. I know how hard it is to explain something like this. Remember I told you that I have a friend who knows I talk to you and she thinks I should stop...because I don't know you, and she also doesn't think that the guy I'm going out with would think too much of my having a mysterious phone friend."

"Is he the jealous type?"

She opened her mouth and then closed it, pursing her lips slightly. "I have no idea. I mean, he's never given me reason to believe he is, but then, maybe he's never had cause . . . you know, I don't think he would be, anyway."

"Why is that?"

"Because I think Nick is too secure in his own sense of self. He's too handsome, for one thing."

He cleared his throat again before asking, "What do you mean?"

"Well, when a man is that good-looking why would any woman risk losing him? I could understand if he were a creep, but Nick is a real gentleman. No, I don't think he'd be the jealous type. In fact, I think I'd be more inclined to be jealous than him."

"Why?"

"Because while I'd never two-time him, I wonder sometimes why he was attracted to me. I'm not beautiful, I'm not really brilliant, I'm not witty, I'm not athletic. . . . Oh, boy, you should have seen the softball game we played today. What a riot. I'm one of the world's worst athletes, but I actually had fun."

"That's the point of a game, isn't it? To have fun?"

Meg nodded to herself. "Yes. That's what Nick said, too. I think I still haven't gotten over how competitive everyone was when I was in school. It was like you were everything if you won, and nothing if you lost. That's a lot of pressure to put on anyone."

"Well, it sounds like everything turned out good, then."

"Oh, it did. But if it hadn't been for Nick and his patience, I don't think it would have. You know, James, I probably shouldn't tell you this, but I really think I'm falling for Nick."

She waited for his quiet laughter or his worried sigh, but neither came. In fact, when thirty seconds had gone by without a peep, she wondered if the connection had been broken.

"James? Are you still there?"

"Yeah," he finally said, his voice low. "I was just, uh, thinking about something."

"Well, what do you think? Am I crazy? Is it too soon to even consider the possibility?"

Another long pause almost had Meg wondering if James was all right. Then she heard him clear his throat. "I'm not sure. Maybe. How can you—or anyone—be sure about something like that?"

Meg squeezed her pillow to her as she cradled the receiver on her shoulder. "I have no idea. All I know is that when I'm with Nick I feel . . . I don't know . . . tingly and warm, all over. I care about what happens to him. And I . . . sometimes fantasize about a future with him. Is that how you feel about your girlfriend?"

"Uh, well, I fantasize a lot."

Meg just laughed out loud. "James, you're awful. Funny, but awful."

"That's me. Awfully funny."

"And awfully sweet. I guess you know that talking with you means a lot to me."

"I like talking with you, too. But, uh, I wish you could pick another word besides sweet to refer to me. That's not very manly."

Laughing at his chagrined tone, Meg acquiesced. "All right. You aren't sweet. You're wonderful. And kind. And considerate."

"Aw shucks, ma'am."

His Brooklyn accent cum Western twang was too much, and Meg giggled into the phone. "That's an amazing accent you've got there, James."

"Yeah, I come from the west side of Brooklyn."

Meg wondered if he was always like this, or only when he was talking with her. She didn't ask but liked to think that it was the latter.

"Sorry to cut this short, James, but it's getting late, and we both have to go to work tomorrow morning."

"I hear you. But I don't mind. My boss is very lenient."

"So's mine," Meg quipped. "Since I'm the boss, there's no one to call me for being late. But sometimes I think I'm harder on myself than a boss would be. Besides, I like to at least try to set a good example for the other employees."

"An admirable trait. Well, I'll let you go. Sleep tight."

"I will. Good night, James. Thanks for calling."

Nick returned his receiver to the cradle and stared at it for several minutes. When his doorbell rang, he lifted the telephone receiver automatically before he scowled at himself and got up to answer the door.

"Hey, Nicky," Gary said, standing in the doorway. "I was wondering if you had some eggs you could lend me for my breakfast tomorrow morning."

"What am I? The corner store?"

Gary shook his head. "Nope. But you are closer than the corner store. If you don't want me borrowing your food and stuff, you shouldn't have taken my advice when I told you about this place. I'm the one who was in the neighborhood first, you know."

Nick sighed and waved his friend in. "Oh, come on in and get the eggs. And you live almost ten blocks from here. You're just too cheap to go to the store."

After he strolled into the apartment, Gary turned and regarded Nick.

"What's wrong? Why do you look so spacey?"

"Because I'm in a mess. Created, of course, by my own doing. So I have no one but myself to blame. Unfortunately, I have no idea how I'm going to get myself out of it."

"I have no idea what you're babbling about, Nick. You lost me back with the eggs."

Nick waved distractedly at the telephone. "I called her again tonight. I knew I shouldn't. I knew I should have just stopped it altogether, but I let my curiosity get the better of me."

"What are you...? Oh, you mean Meg? Your alter ego James called her again? What a racket. I think this could be a major achievement in dating, you know."

"Well, I'm going to be lucky to come out of this in one piece. It isn't just interesting tidbits I'm picking up anymore, Gary, it's gone into a whole other realm. Do you have any idea what she told me tonight? What she told James, that is?"

Gary shook his head and sat down in an armchair to watch Nick pace. "No, and if it's kinky, don't leave anything out."

Nick shot him a withering look, then shoved his hands into his pockets. "She told me she was falling for me, for Pete's sake! But she thought she was telling James."

"Whoo-ee," Gary said. "I didn't realize that you two were that serious. No, I take that back. I could see you headed in a serious direction, I just hadn't realized that you'd gotten there yet."

"Neither had I."

"So she's falling for you. It's not like it's a news flash...or is it? You don't feel the same way?"

Nick thought about all the times they'd gone out, all the times he'd kissed her and held her. They'd talked about so much... Actually, he thought with chagrin, they'd done most of their talking when he'd been James.

"I don't know. I think maybe I do. But that isn't the problem."

"I still don't see that you have a problem. You stop calling her as James, tell her you want to be exclusive, and take it from there.

Nick scratched his jaw uncertainly. He wasn't as convinced. "It can't be that easy. You don't understand Meg. She's really a shy person, and she doesn't talk about her feelings easily. To James, she pours out her heart and tells him her fears and doubts. To me, she's not as open. Yet. I was hoping that she'd transfer her trust from him to me."

"But you are he. I mean you are you. I mean...you know what I mean. She really tells James stuff she doesn't tell you?"

"Yes. That's how I've managed to get her to open up and not be so shy."

Gary looked as if he wasn't quite sure if he was following the play by play. "Doesn't it bother you that your girlfriend—the woman you now say you want to be more serious with—will tell things to a stranger over the phone that she won't tell you?"

Nick had tried not to think about that much, but lately it had been doing just that...bothering him. "I guess so. I just thought that she'd give up telling James so much when she felt she could trust me enough. But now she says she's falling for me, but she still doesn't tell *me*, she tells *James*."

"But you are James!"

"She doesn't know that. And I can't tell her. I think she would be too hurt to ever trust me again."

Gary shrugged and stood up, headed for the kitchen. "So, don't ever tell her. Men have a right to keep a few secrets of their own, you know. But I wouldn't call her anymore as James. It worked for a while, but I don't think you should risk a relationship over it."

Nick smiled weakly at him. "You're a pretty good friend when you try, buddy."

"I know," he smiled immodestly. "Besides, if I weren't, you wouldn't let me come over at midnight to borrow eggs."

"How are you doing, Mrs. Brodsky?"

"Just fine, Meg. Is my book in?"

Meg reached under the counter and pulled out the paperback mystery novel. "Yes, it's right here."

"Oh, good. That woman sure knows how to describe a murder, doesn't she?"

Meg just smiled. The thought of little old Mrs. Brodsky getting into homicides was somehow not as incongruous as it should have been. "I suppose she must, Mrs. Brodsky, or you wouldn't keep buying her books."

The old woman laughed and hitched her purse up to the crook of her elbow. "That's right. I'll be right back, dear, I want to get a book for my youngest grandson for his birthday."

As the woman wandered away toward the back of the store, Meg was nudged by Shawn. "So you told your phone friend how you feel about Nick, but you haven't told Nick. Doesn't this move you to ask of yourself what's wrong with this picture?"

"I know, I know," Meg sighed. "It's just that . . . I guess I'm a little afraid of his reaction. Besides, what's the big hurry?"

Shawn shrugged. "None, I guess. Although I don't know how you can see him all the time and not tell him."

"It isn't easy. Sometimes I just want to blurt it right out."

"So why don't you?"

"What if he doesn't feel the same? I would be a basket case for weeks. I mean, how humiliating. Pour your heart out to a man, only to have him say nothing? Or worse, to squirm or laugh."

Shawn's brown eyes narrowed. "You've never told any-one you loved them, have you? Of course not, you've never even been in love before."

Meg shook her head. "I take it you have?"

"Oh, lots of times. Well, I thought I was. But I wasn't really. Sometimes it takes me a while to catch on to what is obvious to everyone else."

Leaning on the counter, Meg regarded her friend wryly. "Maybe we should take a trip into the self-help section and read up on women who love men but won't tell them be-cause they aren't sure what kind of men they really are."

Shawn seemed to ponder this seriously. "No. We'd be just as well off in the science fiction/fantasy section."

"Speaking of the fantastic, when is the next Splerb Veeblie game?"

"I'm glad you asked. Gary called me earlier today, and it's tomorrow night. I told him that it would help if we could get a schedule. He said that the Veeblies are very unpredict-able, but generally to leave Tuesdays and Thursdays free, just in case."

Meg couldn't help but smile at the memory of the scruffy bunch of ball players. "They're a dedicated, disciplined group, those Veeblies."

"Don't get smart," Shawn warned. "Since we are now Splerb Veeblies, I don't think we should be so high and mighty."

The next night, Meg had to agree, as she wore her new Splerb Veeblie shirt and a pair of stretchy bicycle pants, that she was just as nutty as the rest of her team.

"You look great," Nick said softly, his eyes skimming down over her decidedly unshy attire.

"Oh, I...um...thanks. The pants were Shawn's idea. She thought we should try to match for the uniform's sake."

Meg didn't believe that Shawn really thought that and hadn't believed it when Shawn had first said it, but she'd given in and worn the skintight pants anyway. Shawn was right about one thing: if they were the only two women on the team, they were going to get stared at occasionally, regardless of what they wore. And Meg felt more comfortable thinking they were watching her rear instead of her front.

"Play ball!"

Out into center field she trudged, not dreading the game in the least. Actually, she'd looked forward to it all day, and was anxious for it to get under way.

Glancing over at Russ, she just laughed. "Don't you think that the lounge chair is pushing it a bit?"

Snapping the chair open with a flourish, Russ sat down and attached a little umbrella to its back. "Nope. Besides, if someone actually hits it out here, I can still get up and catch it."

Meg just shook her head and looked back toward the action—at least, what would have been the action if anyone had actually hit the ball, which they didn't. The other team was, if possible, worse than the Splerb Veeblies. They were defeated soundly and claimed they were jinxed because the Veeblies had women on the field.

"You're just jealous," Gary taunted, "because you can't get any women to play with you."

Nick shook his head in mock despair at Gary. Then he turned and looked at Meg and Shawn. "Isn't he a gracious winner?"

"Gracious?" Gary gaped. "Who needs grace when you win? Grace is for when you lose. Besides, those pinheads beat the hell out of us last time and then laughed at us." He turned to yell after the vanquished team, "May you all develop the need for root canals!"

"Ouch," Shawn winced. "You mean it when you curse somebody, don't you?"

"That's right. Keep it in mind. Now, are we going to eat, or what? I am in danger of starving to death."

They all made disparaging remarks about Gary's endless appetite, and then went out to dinner.

When they emerged from the restaurant, Gary took Shawn home in his car, and Nick took Meg home in his.

"You're so lucky to have a car." Meg sighed as she leaned back comfortably in Nick's car, the sun roof and windows open, her hair whipping wildly around her face.

"Sometimes I don't feel so lucky," Nick replied. "Parking fees are outrageous, and so are insurance rates. And I never drive it when I'm going into the city."

"Why not?"

"Because the subway is so much easier and more convenient. And there's never any place to park once you get there. But I like having the car for running around on weekends and for things like the ball games. Once a month or so I drive out to visit my parents in Sound Beach."

"I think you like it because of the freedom it affords," Meg said. "That's why I would like a car. Just to be able to get into it and drive anywhere you want, no matter how far away it is or what time of day it is."

"That's true. So why don't you get one?"

Meg sighed and turned her head toward the passing street signs. "Because every spare dollar I have is saved so that I can buy my parents' house."

Nick nodded. "Oh, yeah. So where is this fabulous house of yours?"

She looked at him and frowned. "It really isn't fabulous, you know. It's just a house. It looks a lot like the other houses around here. But it's special to me in so many ways, I wouldn't know how to begin to tell you about it."

Nick reached over to grab Meg's hand and squeeze it. "I didn't mean to sound flippant about your house. I know it's special to you. Come on, where is it? I want to see it."

Meg hesitated. "Are you sure?"

"Of course, I'm sure."

"All right," she smiled, and gave him directions to the quiet neighborhood where she'd grown up. "It's right up there on the right," she said as they neared the house. "The one with the blue shutters."

Nick parked the car at the curb, ignoring the No Parking sign, and turned off the engine.

Meg drank in the sight of the house. Most of her hopes and dreams and worries for the past year and a half had revolved around this one house. Until Nick had come into her life, nothing had been more important to her.

"I know it doesn't look like a dream house," she told him, "but it is just that to me. I've loved that house since we first moved into it almost fourteen years ago. It just...I don't know...it spoke to me, it enveloped me, it protected me. And it's where I want to live."

Nick peered through the windshield at the house. "I think I know what you mean. Although I've never felt that way about a house myself, I've wanted a house for much those same reasons. But ever since I went to college, I've always lived in an apartment, and there isn't much point in buying a house until I need one."

Meg was about to ask him at what point he thought he'd need one. But then she realized that most people bought houses when they married or wanted to have a family. If he wasn't ready for that, then she wasn't going to ask him why not.

"I don't need it," Meg admitted. "But I do want it. And I might need it someday."

"Yeah, me, too," Nick said. "This is the kind of house I think I'd want, too. It's really quiet on this street, isn't it?"

Meg nodded. "That's one of the reasons I like it so much. It's near the city, but the city isn't obvious here."

"And it's probably a great place for parking in the summertime."

Nick's hand crept across her waist and flicked her seat belt open. He then tugged her into his arms and kissed her warmly, his lips sliding against hers with gentle insistence. Meg was only too happy to let his mouth manipulate hers, and did some manipulating of her own.

When his hand touched her breast, Meg surprised herself by leaning into his caress. Usually when a man tried to touch her breasts, she drew back, the caress bringing back memories of gropes she'd rather forget. But with Nick, everything was different. She wanted Nick to touch her, to desire her body. For the first time in her life, she didn't regret her build. If Nick liked her the way she was, she was glad for it.

"Hey, what are you kids doing? We don't put up with that kind of behavior around here. Do your parents know where you are and what you're doing? Why, you ought to be ashamed, right out here in the open."

They broke apart at the sound of the man's voice, and Nick had started the car and was halfway down the street before he looked over to see Meg laughing.

"What?"

"That was Mr. McGruder. He's been pulling that exact same thing for as long as I can remember. He lives in the house next door to mine. He leans out his upstairs window and scares people all the time. Then he chuckles to himself when they run."

Nick laughed. "I guess I'm too conditioned. If you're making out and someone yells at you, you run."

"Too conditioned? You do this sort of thing all the time, then, do you?"

"Well, not as much as I used to," he admitted. "But now that you've reminded me about how much fun it is, I may have to do it more often."

Meg smiled even as she blushed and opened her mouth to tell him that she loved him, but shut it as he stopped in front of her building and looked at her.

"Would you like to come up for a while?" Meg asked softly.

Nick's smile hit Meg right in the pit of her stomach. "I'd love nothing better. But unless you want to cook breakfast for me, I don't think I should."

Her mouth went dry and her heart fluttered wildly at the implication of his words. But, as much as the thought thrilled her, Meg knew she wasn't ready to take such an important step, even with Nick, even though she loved him.

"Oh, Nick, I..."

When she couldn't seem to get any words out in intelligible order, Nick just leaned over and kissed her. "It's all right. I didn't expect you to say, 'Yeah, sure, come on up.'"

"What *did* you expect?"

"I don't know. I guess I figured you'd want to think about it. Make sure it's what you really want, that you care enough for me, and that it's right for you."

Meg wrapped her arms around his neck and pulled him to her in a fierce hug. "You are so wonderful, Nick." She pulled back far enough to look at him. "And I'm glad you're not pushing me. That means a lot. I do want it to be perfect. And Nick...I do care for you enough...more than enough. I just..."

"I understand, Meg. And believe it or not, I don't want to rush it, either. Now, come on, I'll walk you up, and then I have to go park the car."

Meg nodded, unable to speak past the lump that had risen in her throat. Nevertheless, she cleared her throat and got out of the car as Nick held the door open.

"I've never had anyone worry about me being able to get up my stairs before," she teased as Nick wrapped his arm around her waist and turned them both toward her downstairs door.

"That's because you never had me around before," he said briefly.

Meg just sighed and leaned into his warm, firm body. No, she'd never had him around before, but if everything worked out, maybe she would have him around from now on.

Chapter Five

Nick was glad that he had seen the movie they were watching, although he hadn't told Meg. He wasn't paying attention to what the characters were doing, as his mind was locked in a furious game of tug of war.

Tell her, don't tell her. Stop calling her, don't stop.

Actually, that wasn't what had him worried, he thought as Meg's fingers curled around his atop the armrest they shared. Just to stop calling probably wouldn't prove difficult, even if he would miss the rapport that James shared with Meg. Frowning, Nick had to admit that that rapport bothered him more and more lately. Meg just wasn't as open about her feelings with him as she was with James, despite the fact that he'd dropped a few less than subtle hints. She would clam up and declare that the subject—generally her—was boring.

No, the loss of the telephone conversations wouldn't be so bad if he thought Meg would simply transfer her confidences to Nick instead of waiting until James called to pour her heart out. His problem was that he didn't think Meg was willing to see him as her confidant while James was still calling. Ergo... no more calls.

Now, could he tell her that he was James? Nick shifted uncomfortably in his seat and glanced over at Meg, who smiled at him before returning her attention to the screen.

No. At least not yet. Meg would likely murder him at this point. If only he could make her forget James.... Groaning softly, Nick swore at himself under his breath. Talk about stupid. Now he wanted her to forget the monster he himself had created. Why did he suddenly empathize with Dr. Frankenstein?

"Is something wrong?"

Nick shook his head at Meg's whispered words. Frankenstein or no, James had breathed his last—and listened to his last—confidence. If Meg had a problem, she could start calling *him*, Nick thought. And after a suitable amount of time had gone by, say ten or fifteen years, maybe he would tell Meg about his little indiscretion.

Years? Nick sat up a little straighter. Since when had he begun to think of his relationship with Meg as—dare he even think it—permanent? A future with Meg? Nick's gaze slid sideways and he took in her profile.

Did the fact that he didn't want to lose her mean that he was falling in love with her? Nick was afraid it might. And that made him more determined than ever to make Meg forget James, the mysterious confidant, and concentrate on Nick, the man she was going out with.

Going out with? That sounded singularly wishy-washy. Maybe he should suggest a more serious commitment? Like what, he thought disgustedly, going steady?

The movie had ended when he wasn't looking, and Nick watched the people in front of them get up and shuffle sideways for the exit aisles.

"That was a good movie, wasn't it?"

Nick nodded. "Yeah, I like spy movies."

"I'm surprised you noticed the spies at all," Meg said as she stood. "You looked sort of preoccupied whenever I looked at you."

Nick rose with her and smiled. "And why were you watching me when you should have been watching the movie?"

The blush that tinged her cheeks made him want to drag her out to the car for a serious session of kissing.

"I always do that," she finally said as they walked up the aisle to the lobby of the movie theater. "I like to know that other people are enjoying the movie, or TV show or play as much as I. I don't do it consciously...."

He took her hand and pushed open the lobby doors as they walked out. "I know you don't," he said quietly as he looked down at her. He doubted that Meg was conscious of many of the unselfish things she did. "I think you just can't bear the thought of not sharing something that you enjoy with whoever is near you."

She smiled sheepishly and shrugged. "I guess you're right. But there is a down side to that, you know. Most of my friends don't like to go to movies with me because I talk during them. Not loud, or anything, but I read so many books and magazines at the store that I am a veritable mine of trivia that I think is interesting and should be shared. Unfortunately most people don't like talking at a movie."

They were at his car, and Nick unlocked the passenger door but didn't open it. Instead he leaned against the car and stared down at Meg. "But you didn't talk to me during the movie. Why was that?"

"I've been trying to restrain myself until I found out if you would mind...besides, you really did seem preoccupied. Are you sure nothing is wrong?"

She was genuinely concerned, Nick thought. And she would, no doubt, lend a sympathetic ear should he need one. So why wouldn't she let him do the same for her?

"Uh, no, nothing's wrong, exactly," he finally said, opening the car door. "I guess I just have a lot on my mind."

Meg just nodded and slid into the car. Nick made his way around to the driver's side and wondered how he could go about getting Meg to open up to him.

"Would you like to go riding with me tomorrow?"

Meg's eyebrows rose as she held the phone to her ear. "Riding?"

"Yeah. Bicycles. In the park. Around the park."

"Sure," she said after a moment. "Why not?"

"You don't sound very enthusiastic."

"I'm sorry," she said, and meant it. "I've just got a lot on my mind right now."

Nick waited, and Meg wondered if she should tell him about the telephone call she'd received earlier. She'd thought about it but wasn't sure if she should bring it up. She'd hoped that James would call. She knew he would understand.

The assumption that James would understand and that Nick might not made her feel guilty, and Meg cleared her throat before she plunged ahead.

"I got a call from my parents earlier, and I'm afraid it's got me down."

"Not bad news, I hope?"

"Not about them, no. But they said that they've decided that they have to sell the house. They want to buy a condo in Florida, and they can't afford it unless they sell the house up here."

"Oh. That's too bad. I guess you're not able to get a mortgage or anything?"

Meg's laugh was almost a sob. "Not hardly."

"Listen, Meg. Come riding with me tomorrow and tell me all about it. It might make you feel better."

Struggling to control her emotions, Meg balked at the thought of sobbing her troubles all over Nick's shoulder. As much as she'd like to, she wasn't sure if Nick would care for it. She liked him so much and she didn't want to scare him off with an emotional outburst. If only James would call, she could get the worst of it out of her system before talking to Nick. Then she wouldn't appear to be such a basket case.

"Meg? Are you still there?"

"Yes, I'm here," she said quickly. Talking out her troubles with Nick was something she shouldn't be reluctant to do, she told herself. He would understand, she told herself. There was nothing to worry about.

Still, she had to force a smile into her voice. "What time should I be ready?"

She wore the skintight bicycle pants Shawn had talked her into buying with an oversized T-shirt knotted over one hipbone, and a pair of running shoes. Meg leaned out of her kitchen window when she heard Nick's voice. She smiled at him across their fire escapes.

He looked eager. "You ready?"

"I'll be right down."

With that she shut her window and grabbed her helmet and water bottle, stuffed her keys in her fanny pack and left.

Her bike was wedged between the stairway and the wall just inside the front door. Not enough space to walk, but just right for a bike. Unfortunately, it wasn't easy getting the bike out of the space and through the door.

She opened the door and propped it open, then went back to unlock and struggle with the bike. Nick peered at her from the stoop.

"What are you doing?"

Meg didn't think that was a very bright question. It should have been obvious that she was wrestling with her bike, trying to get it out of the stairwell.

"I'm getting my bike."

She heard a sigh, then Nick's hand wrapped around her upper arm. "Let me."

As soon as Meg stepped back, Nick grabbed the bike's frame, gave a twist and pulled it straight up over his head. He then proceeded to carry it out to the sidewalk and prop it up next to his own.

He looked back at Meg, an expectant expression on his face. Meg merely shut the door and locked it. She then handed her water bottle to Nick, who strapped it on the bike.

"Got your sunglasses?"

Meg nodded and reached for the zipper to her fanny pack. "Yep. Right here. These little things are handy, aren't they?"

Nick nodded as he watched her put her sunglasses on, and then smiled. "Handy. But you aren't supposed to wear it in the front. It's a fanny pack. It's supposed to rest on your fanny."

Meg looked down. "I know. But it's easier to have it in the front."

"But if it's in the front, it can't draw attention to your rear."

Her head jerked up to find a perfectly serious Nick considering her fanny pack and her fanny from the side.

"Maybe I don't want to draw attention to my fanny," she said.

Nick shrugged. "Suit yourself. But a fanny as nice as yours deserves attention."

Meg felt herself coloring, then laughed. He was doing it on purpose, just to get her to blush. "Get on your bike, you...you rogue."

His eyebrows shot up. "Rogue?"

Meg just smiled and went to mount her bike. "Yes, rogue. An underused but often appropriate word."

Nick got on his bike and they started slowly down the sidewalk. "So I'm branded a rogue. Just because I commented on your fanny?"

Meg tried not to laugh. "Yes."

"What would you call me if I commented on how great your legs look in those pants?"

"Don't be ridiculous." Her words were scolding, but her tone was teasing.

Nick maneuvered his bike next to hers. "What's ridiculous? That you have great legs, or that I *said* you have great legs?"

Meg gazed at his profile, trying to determine if he was making fun of her or not. When he suddenly turned and smiled at her, she knew he was serious. Or at least as serious as the situation warranted. Nick meant every word he said. The sparkle in his eyes and the directness of his gaze told Meg everything she needed to know.

"What's ridiculous is this conversation."

He smiled. "Okay. You don't want to talk about your legs? How about my legs?"

Meg looked over at his tightly muscled thighs, pumping slowly up and down as he pedaled the bike. He wore bicycle pants, as well, so that every movement of those thighs was discernible. Meg didn't think that she should tell Nick what she really thought about his legs. So she just shrugged.

"They'll do."

Nick sputtered in mock indignation, and Meg laughed. Then she accelerated, ignoring his dire threats of retaliation.

She realized then that she felt better than she had since her parents had called. And more than that, Nick made her feel better about herself than any man she'd ever met.

Except, maybe, James.

"Ready for a break?"

Meg was still gasping for breath and just stared at Nick, who was barely breathing heavily. He grinned and wheeled his bike off the path onto the grass near a park bench.

Meg just followed him, hoping she didn't fall off her bike before she was able to stop it and alight.

"That was a pretty good workout. Not as far as I usually go, but I knew you probably wouldn't be up for a long one. It wasn't too much for you, was it?"

Upending her water bottle, Meg just held up her other hand. She drained the remaining water from the bottle, then dragged the back of her hand across her lips and shook her head. "Nah, it wasn't too much. Not if you're training for the Olympics. Whatever happened to our relaxing little ride around the park?"

Nick's eyes widened innocently. "We rode around the park."

"We raced around the park," Meg corrected. "I thought we were being chased by a gang of thugs for a while. And I came very close to freaking out when you almost ran down that little old lady."

"I did not. She didn't see me and I could've avoided her in any case. Besides, she should have known she was on the bike path and watched where she was going."

"On our first day out, Shawn and I saw how some of those killer bikers speed along those paths." Meg laughed. "I can tell you that I never really thought that you would be one of them."

Nick opened his mouth to say something, and then stopped. His expression was almost comical in its indecision. "Meg, you should have said something if—"

"I'm kidding," Meg blurted. She couldn't stand the thought of Nick feeling guilty about dragging her around with him against her will. "And I am having a good time, Nick," she insisted, and was rewarded when the concern left his face and he smiled at her.

"Are you sure? You're not just saying you like riding because I own a bike shop and spend a lot of my time riding?"

Her eyes rolled and Meg laughed again. "I'm sure. It's just that it might have been more enjoyable for me if you hadn't set the pace on the previous world record."

Nick shrugged and grinned at her. "Sorry. I'm not used to holding back. When I do something, I tend to go all out. The rewards are greater that way."

Not sure if his innuendo was intentional or not, Meg ignored it. "Well, next time, you can go all out without me trying to keep up with you. I swear, I'm going to be sore from earhole to appetite, as my grandmother used to say. At least I'm a little limbered up from riding with Shawn three days a week. But my poor body isn't used to this kind of punishment."

"Sore? If that's the case, then the least I can do is offer my expertise as a masseur for the evening."

Startled blue eyes narrowed at the mischievous grin on Nick's face. Meg shook her head in mock despair. "As much appeal as the idea has for me at this moment, I fear that I don't know you well enough to let you massage the part of me that would most likely be in need of...um... massaging."

Nick groaned and pulled her into his arms. "Since you've put the quietus on my plans for the evening, you'll have to placate me."

Looping her arms around his neck, Meg tilted her head back and smiled at him. "Placate you? And how would you suppose I could do that?"

He smiled. "Well, since we're standing in the park in the middle of the day with who knows who's watching, I'll settle for a kiss."

Meg was glad that she'd had time to recover her breath, because she needed it. She tugged gently on Nick's neck and he obligingly bent to meet her lips.

Considering where they were, Meg thought the kiss was almost indecent. Their bodies touched, but their hands were respectable. Meg kept hers around Nick's neck and Nick kept his resting on Meg's back.

Not being able to touch each other more, or to deepen the kiss, they finally broke apart and just stared at each other for a moment.

"Eee-yeuw."

They looked down and over behind the park bench. There, standing and staring at them, were two little boys. Meg figured them to be about six or seven.

Nick scowled at them. "What's the matter?"

"That's gross," one of them said.

The other, perhaps younger, said, "They do it on TV alla time. Big deal."

"Still gross."

Nick looked at Meg, then back at the two boys. He smiled. "It may be gross, guys, but it's a whole lotta fun."

Meg laughed as the two boys expressed their disbelief and ran off in the direction of an adult voice calling their names. Nick laughed and turned to Meg.

"Ready to head back home?"

"I don't know if I should go back with you," she said warily. "You might have cooties, or something."

With that, she ran to her bike and jumped on it.

"Cooties? I'll show you cooties."

Meg hoped none of the adults they passed could hear what they were yelling and laughing about as they rode out of the park, but the kids would understand. Cooties are a dangerous and serious affliction.

Having a boyfriend wasn't something that Meg Porter was well acquainted with. The embarrassingly small number of dates she'd had since she'd been allowed to start dating had been just that. Dates. None had ever gone beyond three or four outings, but now Meg was reveling in what had only been wistful longings to her a few months ago. An exclusive relationship with a man she was falling in love with.

Meg wondered whimsically what the difference was between falling in love and being in love, then decided that it didn't matter. If she was falling, the trip was wonderful, and if she was already there, it was better than she'd ever imagined.

The only problem was that James hadn't called her in more than two weeks. Meg missed talking with him. She wondered if maybe he'd tried to call one of the nights she'd been out with Nick.

"What are you looking so worried about?"

The sound of Nick's voice jolted her out of her musings, and Meg flushed guiltily at having been caught thinking about one man while having dinner with another.

"I...um...actually, I was wondering what had happened to a, uh, friend of mine I haven't heard from in a while. I'm not worried exactly, just curious."

Nick's eyes narrowed into a scowl. "Great. You're thinking about other guys while you're out with me."

"It isn't like that, Nick. And why do you think it's a man? I have more female friends than male friends, you know. At least I did before I joined the Splerb Veeblies."

His gaze didn't wander. "But it wasn't a woman you were thinking about, was it?"

Meg's expression was clouded with confusion. How could he know ... or was he really just guessing?

"No, it wasn't a woman. But neither is it anyone I've ever been out with, or for that matter, ever even seen."

She expected him to gape at her in astonishment or at least bewilderment, but Meg didn't expect Nick to say nothing. The skin across his cheekbones seemed taut and his jaw was clenched, and Meg feared he was really angry. She'd been afraid that something like this might happen if she mentioned James.

Finally he looked over at her plate. "Are you finished?"

Meg just nodded. She had finished eating but didn't think that their discussion was near over. And she wasn't sure she wanted it to continue, even though she knew it should. It was long past time she told Nick about James. But every time she'd considered it, she rejected the idea. Now it seemed that she'd been right. If Nick really was angry, Meg was afraid this could prompt their first real argument.

Too curious to wait once they were in the car, headed for home, she ventured to question Nick about his attitude when he seemed quieter than usual. "Are you angry with me, Nick? About that friend of mine? I can explain—"

Nick shook his head. "No, I'm not angry with you. But I do think we need to talk about this. And not in the car. And not at your place. The only thing being in your tiny apartment with you makes me think about is you. And me. And your hide-a-bed."

Meg was thankful for the darkness that hid her reddened cheeks from his gaze. Not that she was embarrassed that he wanted her. She wanted him, too. But saying it or hearing it still made her blush.

She didn't notice that he'd pulled into the parking lot of a bar until they were parked. Looking around, she almost groaned aloud. Why this place?

"Come on," Nick said as he held her door open. "Maybe we can find a quiet booth."

Following him reluctantly, Meg almost blurted out the assurance that they would be able to find a booth. The few times she'd been there with Greg, there had always been open booths. A weekend night might be different, but nine o'clock on a Tuesday wasn't the happy hour.

Inside the tavern-style bar, it was busier than it had looked from the outside, but there were a few booths available, and Nick headed for the one farthest from the bar traffic. Meg, her fingers securely entwined with Nick's, didn't protest, although she did look around more than he did.

She spotted Bill Ferguson at the bar, and Meg saw him frown at her, as if trying to remember who she was. She fixed her eyes ahead of her and hoped he didn't remember. She didn't want Nick to know about the night that Greg had dumped her in this bar.

That was the same night she'd first talked to James, Meg thought as she slid into the booth across from Nick.

"This place isn't too bad," Nick was saying. "Ever been here? It's not too far from us."

"I've been here a few times, but not recently."

A waitress came and took their orders. The amount of time it took them to decide what to have made Meg realize that neither of them was really interested in having drinks.

"So tell me about this friend of yours you don't know."

His calmly spoken words caught Meg unaware, and she wasn't sure how much she should tell him. Then she firmly told herself that this was Nick and that it was high time she told him about James, even if he did think she was weird. It wasn't right to keep something like that hidden. She only hoped he didn't become angry.

"I—that is, I do know him. We've just never met."

Nick just sat there. Waiting.

The waitress brought their drinks, and Meg played with her glass after taking a small sip. Then she looked up at Nick. "He's like a pen pal. Sort of. Only without the pen. I'm not explaining this very well, am I?"

Nick's smile looked strained. "I'm sure you'll get better."

"It's really rather funny, when you think about it," she offered reluctantly. "I'd come home after a disastrous date, and a wrong number called and I ended up talking with him. I know it sounds crazy, but that's what happened. Go ahead and tell me how stupid I am—Shawn did—but it won't change the fact that I don't think that James is an ax murderer and I like talking to him. And I don't want to stop talking to him, though that may be a moot point, since he hasn't called me in over two weeks."

That said, she leaned back and took a long sip of her wine cooler. Then she looked up at Nick, who just watched her with an enigmatic expression. Then he leaned forward and put his forearms on the table between them.

"I didn't say you were stupid. But I wonder what you could find to talk about with a stranger for…how long have you, uh, been talking with him?"

"Oh, a few months. And I'm never at a loss for things to talk about to James. Anything and everything. He never puts me down or laughs at me."

Nick took a long sip of his drink and then set it on the table where he cradled the glass between his hands, rolling it back and forth as he alternately watched it and Meg.

"Do you think you might want to meet this guy someday?"

Meg's eyes widened. "No, of course not."

Nick met her open gaze and shrugged one shoulder. "Why not? I mean, if he's so great to talk to?"

It wasn't easy to find the right words to describe what she felt for James. She began slowly. "James is not like a real

AN IMPORTANT MESSAGE FROM THE EDITORS OF SILHOUETTE®

Dear Reader,

Because you've chosen to read one of our fine romance novels, we'd like to say "thank you"! And, as a **special** way to thank you, we've selected <u>four more</u> of the <u>books</u> you love so well, **and** a Victorian Picture Frame to send you absolutely *FREE!*

Please enjoy them with our compliments...

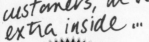

Senior Editor,
Silhouette Romance

P.S. And <u>because</u> we value our customers, we've attached something extra inside ...

EDITOR'S
**FREE
GIFT
SEAL**
THANK YOU

PEEL OFF SEAL AND PLACE INSIDE

HOW TO VALIDATE YOUR
EDITOR'S FREE GIFT
"THANK YOU"

1. Peel off gift seal from front cover. Place it in space provided at right. This automatically entitles you to receive four free books and a lovely pewter-finish Victorian picture frame.

2. Send back this card and you'll get brand-new Silhouette Romance™ novels. These books have a cover price of $2.69 each, but they are yours to keep absolutely free.

3. There's no catch. You're under no obligation to buy anything. We charge nothing–ZERO–for your first shipment. And you don't have to make any minimum number of purchases–not even one!

4. The fact is thousands of readers enjoy receiving books by mail from the Silhouette Reader Service™ months before they're available in stores. They like the convenience of home delivery and they love our discount prices!

5. We hope that after receiving your free books you'll want to remain a subscriber. But the choice is yours–to continue or cancel, anytime at all! So why not take us up on our invitation, with no risk of any kind. You'll be glad you did!

6. Don't forget to detach your FREE BOOKMARK. And remember...just for validating your Editor's Free Gift Offer, we'll send you FIVE MORE gifts, *ABSOLUTELY FREE!*

YOURS FREE!
*This lovely Victorian pewter-finish miniature is perfect for displaying a treasured photograph–and it's yours **absolutely free**–when you accept our no-risk offer!*

person to me, Nick. His voice is real and his thoughts and feelings are real, but since he can't see me or touch me, the reality of him is once removed. I feel...safe when I talk with him. He makes me feel better about myself because he's always supportive and never judgmental. He doesn't really know who I am or what I look like, and I am equally ignorant about him. He calls me every so often and we talk.''

Nick just nodded. ''But he hasn't called you lately?''

''No, he hasn't.''

''And you wish he would?''

Meg didn't think she liked the direction in which this conversation was headed. ''Well, yes, I guess I do.''

''Why haven't you ever told me about this guy you talk to, Meg?''

The words were slightly accusatory, but his eyes held almost a burning curiosity. Meg felt herself wondering why he wasn't angry instead of curious.

''I guess I thought you wouldn't understand, or that you would be angry. Aren't you?''

''Angry? No. I think I'm more interested to know what you talked about and why you felt the need to talk with a stranger.''

He *is* angry, Meg thought. He just won't admit it. ''What we talked about isn't important, Nick. And after that first time, I've never felt that James was a stranger.''

''Did you talk about me?''

Softly uttered, but with a measure of steel behind them, Meg knew his words weren't to be ignored or brushed away. She met his eyes and saw that he knew the answer before she spoke. ''You did,'' he said quietly. ''And yet you want me to believe that it shouldn't be important to me that you speak with him?''

''I didn't mean it that way,'' Meg protested. ''And it's difficult to describe how I can talk with James. He listens, but doesn't try to tell me what to do. Shawn said that he was sort of a telephone psychiatrist."

"He's harmless." Nick nodded.

"I suppose so," Meg agreed.

"What I mean is that you have nothing to fear from him because he can't hurt you. What did you tell him about me?"

Meg shifted in her seat. "Nothing derogatory."

Nick leaned closer. "Have you told him anything you haven't told me?"

Swallowing was suddenly a difficult proposition. Meg forced the last of her beverage down her throat and met Nick's searching gaze. "Yes, I guess I have, but—"

"Why?"

"Why what?"

"Why do you tell him things you don't feel you can tell me? Or more to the point, is it because you don't feel you can tell me everything?"

Meg frowned. "No one has to tell the person they're ... going out with ... everything."

"I didn't mean everything under the sun. I just want to know why you feel you can't tell me the kinds of things you tell your phone friend."

His reaction to all of this was mystifying to Meg. He wasn't angry, or remonstrative or even really very surprised. He just seemed curious. More than that, she thought, he seemed to need to probe into her reasons for what she'd done. Rather than ask her to explain *what* she'd done, Nick seemed to want to know why she'd done it. And the why of it all was something that Meg was still trying to ascertain for herself.

"I'm not sure I can answer your questions, Nick," Meg finally said. "Not because I won't, but because I'm not sure I've figured out the answers for myself."

Nick inclined his head to the right and continued to watch her. "Will you tell me one thing?" When she nodded hesitantly, he said, "Do you trust me?"

"Of course I do," Meg blurted out, then grimaced when one dark eyebrow arched sardonically. "All right, maybe it seems as if I don't. I don't trust easily, Nick. But I'm willing to try to be more open with you. Actually, I have been more open with you than I have been with other men."

His smile reached out for her, and Meg leaned over the table toward him. "I think I know that, Meg. And I don't mean to criticize you or your friend. I just want to think that you would trust me enough to confide in me and tell me the kinds of things you would tell your other friend."

Meg's smile grew stronger and she was about to reassure him that she trusted him more than any other man she'd ever met, when she saw someone step up next to their table. Looking up, she saw that it was Bill Ferguson. And from the look on his face, Meg knew that he'd finally remembered who she was.

"Hello, Bill," she said uncertainly. She gestured at Nick and introduced them. Bill just nodded as he looked from Meg to Nick and back.

"I haven't seen you in here since…well, since the last time I saw you."

Meg chuckled, surprising herself as much as Bill. "No, I guess you haven't. I've been pretty busy."

"Yeah, I guess. Anyway, I just thought I'd say hello and tell you that while you might not be a regular here, you-know-who still is."

Meg didn't need to look at Nick to know that he was curious about this whole exchange. But she would explain after Bill had left. Smiling up at Bill, she shrugged. "I suppose that might have bothered me once, but it doesn't anymore."

Bill's smile was decidedly lopsided. "Well, that's good to hear, since he just came in about five minutes ago."

With that Bill was gone, and Meg tried to smile at Nick and pretend nothing had happened. But he wasn't having any of it.

"Who's 'he'?"

Meg's eyes darted around the bar before she could stop them, and she saw where Greg Bayer sat at a table with Jerri Jacobs. They looked very cozy. Meg thought it interesting that she felt very detached. It was like looking at two strangers. Which was, essentially, what they were.

"'He' is a guy I came in here with a few times before I met you. Bill remembers me because of an unfortunate incident that marked the end of the last date Greg and I had."

Nick's eyes followed hers, and when Meg looked back at him, he turned his head to look at her. "An old boyfriend?"

Was he jealous? Meg thought that was funny. Especially since he seemed more jealous of Greg than he had of James, and there was certainly more cause there than there was where Greg was concerned. "No, he was never my boyfriend. We just went out a few times. Actually, I was never all that attracted to him, but he kept telling me how taken he was with me, so I went out with him."

"So, what 'unfortunate incident' marked the end of your relationship?"

"We never had anything that resembled a relationship," she told him. "And I'd rather not talk about what happened."

Nick's eyes narrowed as Meg's dropped to her empty glass. "Why do I get the feeling that if my name were James, you would tell me more about this?"

Her head shot up and she stared at him. He was right, of course. Meg sighed her frustration. "I'm sorry. You're right. Actually, James already knows what happened. Our first conversation was on the night of the incident." Taking a deep breath, Meg clasped her hands in her lap. "Greg and I were on a date. We came here. He excused himself to go to the rest room. The next thing I knew, Bill was telling me that Greg was leaving. The last time I saw Greg, he was walking out the front door with Jerri. That's the girl he's with now."

Nick looked from Meg to where Greg and Jerri sat. "That guy left you to leave with *her?* What a jerk."

Meg laughed. And was so very glad that she didn't have to force it. Now that she'd found someone who was so much better than Greg, it all seemed very funny.

"Just be glad I didn't meet you the night I left here. I was bound and determined to lay low any man who crossed my path. It's a wonder James stayed on the line at all after I yelled at him for being a man when he called."

"Why didn't you just hang up?"

Meg sat back and regarded him. "I did, actually, but he called back. That time I didn't. And I'm not really sure why I didn't hang up again. Maybe because he had a cold and sounded so pathetic. Or maybe it was his Brooklyn accent. Maybe it was both. A Brooklyn accent with a cold was too interesting to hang up on. Besides, I think he just said the right thing when I needed to hear it."

Nick just nodded then and asked her if she was ready to leave. Meg agreed and rose to lead the way out, deliberately walking past Greg and Jerri's table, where she paused just long enough to cause him to look up, then she sailed past him and out of the bar.

"What was that all about?" Nick asked as they got into his car.

"I just wanted to see what he'd do."

"He looked sort of sick to me."

"Yeah. That's the best he's ever looked to me."

Chapter Six

The next week flew by in a whirl for Meg. There was a special promotion going on at the store, which had her and Shawn running to keep up with the customers and the distributors; the Splerb Veeblies won another softball game, which had Gary crowing about their unbeatable team; and Nick had either seen her or called her every day.

Visiting his other bike store on Sunday, Meg saw that Nick was very proud of his accomplishments, and rightly so. The shop was similar to the one next to her bookstore, except that it was bigger. There were several hundred bicycles dangling from the ceiling, not to mention the hundreds more on the floor. There was a repair center on the premises, and all around the sales floor there were posters and information about various places to bike and races that were being held.

She understood the amount of work he had to put into the shops, and Meg realized why it was that he so often excused himself to work at the Queens location. Nick had to have distinct workaholic tendencies, although he did take time out for her and the Veeblies. She watched him as he showed off his shop, and Meg could see the vitality that fueled his ambitions and made him believe he could have anything he wanted.

Meg sometimes felt that sort of invincibility, although not too often, and never in the midst of a promotion. This time it was a midsummer sale. It was the Saturday before the fourth of July and the store was filled with people who wanted to buy something to read on the beach, or at the lake.

"Meg, do we have any more of Dave Barry's latest book?"

"I just put the dump up yesterday."

Donna, one of the store's part-time booksellers, just shrugged. "It's empty now."

"I'll go get the other dump. I'm glad I ordered two."

Two minutes after she replaced the cardboard display of books in the front of the store, Meg was prevailed upon for her opinion of three potential gifts, none of which she'd read. Quoting from reviews from the *Times* might not be exactly honest, but it satisfied the customer, and Meg turned to head behind the counter, where Shawn and Donna were ringing up sales.

"Meg, a woman just asked about some business book she'd read an article about. She wants us to mail it out. I would have gone with her to look, but the line was too long."

"I'll go. Do a sales figure check when you get the chance, okay, Shawn?"

"Sure thing."

Meg headed back to the business section, where she found a young woman peering at the titles.

"Can I help you find something?"

The woman looked up and smiled. "I hope so. My brother is thinking about putting a computer system in his business, and I thought I'd get him a few books. One in particular I read about in *Business Week* magazine."

A folded page, ripped from the magazine, was pulled from her purse, and the woman showed it to Meg, who recognized the book as new and was glad they'd gotten a few copies.

"Yes, that's right over here," she said, walking around the freestanding bookcase to pull the book from the top shelf.

"Oh, good. And the other book I was thinking about was just a general computer book that listed different systems and their capabilities and costs. I have no idea if there even is such a book, really."

Meg walked two shelf units down and scanned the titles in the general computer section. "This might be what you're looking for," she said, pulling a book down. "Or this one," she pointed. "I'm afraid those are the only ones we have right now."

The woman flipped through the table of contents of both books and nodded. "I think this one will be all right."

Meg replaced the other book and walked back toward the cash registers with the woman. "Did my assistant say something about your wanting to mail these?"

"Oh, yes. I'm going to be out of town for the next month, and these books are for my brother's birthday, which isn't for another two weeks, but since I won't be able to be here for it, I wanted to surprise him with the books."

Meg stepped behind the counter and took the books from the woman. There was a momentary lull on the line of people and Donna announced that she was going to take her break before the next wave hit, then disappeared into the back room.

"Now, I'll need the name and address of the person you're mailing these to, and any special instructions."

"Oh, I guess I should put a card in with them, shouldn't I?"

While Meg started to ring up the books, the woman plucked a birthday card from a nearby rack and hastily wrote a message in it.

"I'd take care to pick out a special card," she said, "but he'll just toss it, anyway."

Meg turned a piece of paper toward the woman, who wrote a name and address on it, then wrote out a check for the books and the mailing charge, which she pushed back to Meg along with her identification.

Writing the numbers automatically, Meg barely noticed the woman's name. Allison Moorhead.

"There you are, Mrs. Moorhead," Meg said as she returned the identification. "We'll make sure these get out this afternoon."

"Oh, there's no hurry," she laughed. "You could just walk them over, since he lives right next door. You probably know him. He owns the bike shop next to you. Nick Morgan. I was just visiting and when I left I saw this store and thought about Nick's birthday. Oh, if you would, please underline the Junior after his name on the envelope. He hates that." She laughed again.

Meg laughed, too, and nodded as she looked down at the name and address the woman had printed. James Nicholas Morgan, Junior.

"I'll be sure he gets it. And I do know Nick."

The woman looked at Meg's name tag. "Meg Porter. Of course, Nicky's mentioned you often. I was wondering when he was going to drag you out to Long Island to meet the family."

Meg smiled. Nick mentioned his family every once in a while, and Meg recalled him telling her he had several brothers and sisters.

"Maybe soon," she told the woman, and began to wonder herself why Nick hadn't taken her to meet his family. After another moment, the woman left and Meg stared down at the form in her hand.

"That's funny," Meg said aloud.

"What is?" Shawn asked.

"That was Nick's sister. She wants us to mail these books to him for his birthday. But look, Nicholas is his middle name. His first name is—"

A cold, sinking feeling invaded Meg's stomach and started to move upward into her chest.

"His first name? Must be pretty bad if he didn't want us to know about it. What is it? Aloysius? Murgatroid?"

Meg stared at the name, then picked up the woman's check and looked at the name, a sense of dread filling her. Allison. Her telephone number was printed on the check. It was identical to Meg's number, except for the last digit.

Shawn waved her hand in front of Meg's pale face. "Hey, what's wrong? What's Nick's name?"

"It's James," Meg whispered.

"Oh. Well, what's so bad about— Oh, my God! He isn't...he can't be...."

Meg turned pain-filled, confused eyes to her friend. "I'm afraid it can be. His sister's name is Allison and her phone number is only one digit different than mine. I remember that when he first called, James referred to his sister Allison. Only when he said it, it sounded like Addison because of his cold."

Shawn looked at the name the woman had printed, and the check, and her mouth tightened. "That rotten creep. And here I was thinking what a great catch he was."

"So was I," Meg said, trying to sound rueful, but her voice caught and she was terribly afraid she might just start sobbing all over the electronic cash registers.

"Shawn, can you handle things by yourself until Donna gets back from her break? It shouldn't be more than ten minutes."

"Sure, no problem. What are you going to do?"

Meg pulled her purse out from beneath the counter and shrugged. "I have no idea. I just want to walk and be by myself right now."

Walking didn't help much, and neither did being by herself. The tears she knew were there refused to fall. With growing dismay, Meg remembered all the things she had told James over the past few months. As she walked, her anger grew in proportion with her hurt. Passing an appliance store, she spotted an item in the window and without giving it her usual thorough consideration, walked in and bought it.

An hour after she left, Meg was back in the bookstore, her jaw set with a gritty sense of determination that caused Shawn to whistle under her breath.

"I thought you were going to go out and cry yourself into a headache. Instead, you come back looking like you're ready to do battle. What's in the bag . . . a gun?"

"No, an answering machine."

Shawn nodded thoughtfully, and just watched as Meg put her purse and the answering machine under the counter and pinned her name badge back on.

"I hope you aren't planning on putting a scathing message on it," Shawn said. "I mean, what if someone else calls? Like your family, or a friend. Or a business type?"

"My family and friends will understand, and anyone wanting to do business with me should be calling me here. I don't want to talk to Nick and unless I don't want to talk to anyone else, I had to get the machine.''

"But Meg," Shawn ventured. "He lives right next door. You can buy an answering machine for the telephone, but you can't help but see him on the sidewalk when you both open the stores every morning.''

Meg had thought about that. "I know. But seeing him doesn't mean I have to talk to him.''

Shawn murmured something noncommittal and turned to help a customer. Meg gathered up a sales report and went into the store to count books. She needed something to keep her mind off her troubles, but she doubted that anything would be able to accomplish that feat.

The new answering machine was installed as soon as she got upstairs after work, right after she made sure the shade on the window facing Nick's apartment was securely down. Meg then picked at the salad she'd prepared for her dinner and tried to concentrate on a new biography that she'd borrowed from the store. Laying the book down with a sigh, Meg knew that her concentration was nil.

Every time the phone rang that evening, Meg jumped and stared at it. Whoever the first caller was hung up without leaving a message. The second caller was Shawn, whose clear voice spoke to her from the machine after the beep had sounded.

"Whoa, boy, am I glad I'm not him. Are you there, Meg? Come on, I know you're there. All right, be a recluse. You might think it's what you want, but it's not. And if you ask me, Nick won't just lie down and accept all of this. I think he's more of a fighter. I'll see you tomorrow. 'Bye.''

The machine clicked off and Meg just stared at it. Maybe Shawn had a point. Why should she be a recluse? Just because she'd been humiliated by a man she thought she'd fallen in love with? Just because everything she thought she'd believed to be true about him was suddenly suspect?

Her gaze remained fixed on the telephone, and Meg wondered why she hadn't fallen apart and sobbed her heart out. She felt strangely detached, as if she were part of a dream and her equilibrium was slightly out of kilter. The sudden shrilling of the telephone caused her to start, but she turned calm eyes on the machine as the second ring ended and the machine clicked on.

"Hello, I'm sorry that I can't come to the phone right now, but if you'll leave your name and number after the beep, I'll return your call as soon as possible. Unless, of course, you are James Nicholas Morgan, Junior. That being the case, I will not return your call, and I would appreciate it if you would not call again. And, just for the record, I think that what you did was reprehensible and unforgivable and that you are a slimeball for doing it."

The beep sounded, and there was a pause. Meg thought that whoever it was was going to hang up when she heard a strangled sort of groan emanating from the speaker on the machine.

"Meg?"

It was Nick. Or was it James? Meg just sat in her armchair and wondered what he could possibly think he could say.

"Meg, I'm sorry. I didn't mean it the way it must seem, I swear. Just give me a chance to explain. Meg? If you don't answer this phone, I'm going to come over and wait outside your door until you either come out or get home."

Meg's chest constricted in momentary panic. She surged to her feet and snatched the receiver off its hook, disengaging the recorder.

"Don't you dare come over here!"

"Meg, just listen to me, I know I was wrong, but I didn't do it intentionally... not at first. You have to believe that."

The worried note she thought she heard in his voice caused Meg to roll her eyes, although those eyes were now filled with tears. "No, Nick, I don't have to believe that. In fact, I think that you've pretty much made it clear that it would be a bad idea for me to trust anyone, especially a man. I'm obviously not a very good judge of character."

"Meg, at least give me a chance to explain and—"

"I can't think of anything that would explain your actions, and I don't want to see you again, Nick."

She had meant to say goodbye, but the words stuck in her throat and she just replaced the receiver as quietly as she could. The phone rang again, almost before she'd removed her hand, and she shut off the speaker so that she couldn't hear the caller's message.

The tears she'd wondered about all day suddenly made their appearance as Meg turned away from the telephone. She'd told him she never wanted to see him again, and she probably wouldn't. He'd hurt her more than she'd thought possible, and that thought was wrenching enough, but along with it was the loss of Nick from her life. And James. Giggling hysterically through her sobs, Meg wondered who she would miss more, Nick or James.

Several minutes later she splashed cold water on her face, but it did little to cool the torment she was suffering on the inside, but it did help calm her exterior. At least, it did until she looked up into her reflection and saw how ravaged her face was from her crying.

She snapped the bathroom light off after brushing her teeth, then went back into her living room/bedroom and pulled the cushions off her sofa, before she pulled out the hide-a-bed and threw a blanket on it. Her pillow was punched more than usual as she tried to get comfortable, but after several minutes she gave up, knowing the effort was futile.

Her eyes were tracing the little circles in the ceiling tiles a few minutes later when she heard a rattling at her kitchen window. Frowning for a moment, Meg thought maybe the wind was rattling the pane. But then she heard it again. It wasn't the wind.

She made her way through the dark apartment to the window. She didn't have to raise the shade to know who it was, but she did. There, standing on her fire escape, tapping on her window, was Nick Morgan. *James* Nicholas Morgan, that was.

Meg stepped away to flip on the overhead light and glared at Nick through her window. She didn't go directly to the window, but remained several feet away as she called out to him in a clear, if not completely steady, voice.

"Go away, Nick. I told you I didn't want to see you and I meant it."

He peered at her through the pane of glass and shook his head. "Hi," he said, his voice sounded muffled through her closed window. "Sorry, but I'm not going away until you agree to talk to me."

"Forget it, Nick. Just leave. I'm not interested in anything you have to say."

"Come on, Meg, be reasonable. I know I hurt you, and I'm sorry. I wish I could change it all, but I can't. Please believe me when I say I wasn't trying to deliberately hurt you. It all just got out of hand."

"Right," Meg practically shouted as she struggled to keep a balance between rationality and hysteria. "Why don't you go and tell it to all your buddies and have a good laugh and just leave me alone? It was a good joke while it lasted, but now it's over."

Nick's hands seemed to be clenched into fists, but Meg couldn't be sure.

"It wasn't a joke! It was never a joke, Meg."

"Hey, buddy, where do you think you are, the Bronx? Shut up or I'll call a cop."

Mr. Pellegrini from the building behind Meg's wasn't exactly a diplomat, Meg thought grimly, but if his method worked, she didn't care.

"Meg!"

"Go away, Nick."

"Beat it, Nick, or I'll call a cop. I don't care if you are from the neighborhood."

"All right, I'm going," Nick finally said. "But don't think this is the end of it, Meg."

Meg and Mr. Pellegrini turned off their lights as Nick climbed back onto his own fire escape and into his apartment. Meg crawled back into bed, and wondered despondently what Nick was planning to do to her next. Maybe he would write a book about the whole adventure. As if being an object of ridicule in Brooklyn Heights wasn't enough, maybe she could be ridiculed all over the country.

Nick didn't care that it was so late...or so early...he continued to lean on the doorbell.

He heard a bumping sound from within the apartment, followed by several garbled curses. He removed his finger from the doorbell and leaned against the doorjamb, his hands stuffed into his pockets. There were several scraping sounds, then a gruff inquiry.

"Who the hell is it?"

"Just open the stupid door and you'll find out."

The door was pulled open and Gary stood inside, his hair standing on end and his expression a cross between a scowl and curiosity.

"Nick, do you have any idea what time it is? I have an early appointment tomorrow morning."

"Sure," Nick grumbled as he shoved past Gary into his friend's apartment. "You'd rather drill holes in a stranger's teeth than listen to a personal crisis in your best friend's life.''

Gary closed his front door and sighed. ''I guess I can spare you a few minutes. Want coffee?''

Nick was already pacing in front of Gary's sofa. ''What difference does it make?''

''None, I guess,'' Gary shrugged. ''Just trying to be hospitable.''

''Well, never mind all that. I need ideas and I need a plan, so start thinking.''

Nodding silently, Gary sank into an overstuffed armchair and dropped his chin into his palm. Nick paced several more times before stopping and glaring at his friend.

''What are you doing? You're not helping.''

''I'm thinking. You told me to think, and that's what I'm doing.''

''And what are you thinking about?''

Gary smiled faintly. ''I was thinking that I'd still be asleep if you hadn't come and woken me up.''

Nick rubbed the back of his neck. ''Well, that's not going to help. You're supposed to be thinking of ways for me to get Meg to listen to me, to realize that I didn't mean it the way she thinks. She hates me, Gary. I swear, I didn't think she'd hate me. I thought she'd be mad, but I didn't think it would be this bad.''

''What in the hell are you babbling about?''

Nick leveled his tired eyes on Gary's. ''Meg found out about the phone thing. That I'm James as well as Nick. I don't know how she found out, but she did.''

Gary's eyes widened. He whistled softly and said, ''Took it bad, did she? I warned you not to tell her.''

''But I didn't tell her,'' Nick protested. ''I just called her tonight and she had this answering machine with a message especially for me on it, basically telling me that she knew and for me to drop dead. Finally she picked up the phone and told me personally to basically drop dead.''

''Whoa. I didn't think she'd get all twisted sideways about it. Didn't you tell her that it wasn't meant—''

''I couldn't tell her anything. She hung up on me. So I climbed over my fire escape onto hers and tried to get her to open her window and talk to me.''

Gary chuckled despite the situation. ''You didn't?''

''I had to. But she still wouldn't listen to me. She thinks I did it on purpose as a big joke on her, or something.''

Wincing at the implication, Gary looked up at Nick, who had resumed his pacing. ''That doesn't sound good, Nick.''

''I know that,'' Nick snapped. ''What I don't know is how I'm going to fix this mess.''

''Yeah. And I guess you really do want to fix it, don't you?''

''Of course I do. What kind of question is that?''

Gary slumped farther into his chair and yawned. ''A rhetorical one, obviously. Okay, now that you know what you want to do, you need a way to do it. A plan, you said.''

''Yes, that is right. I'm glad you're finally with me.''

Gary nodded and blocked another yawn with the back of his fist. ''Why don't you just keep calling and going to her apartment? Shouldn't be hard since you live so close. Sooner or later, she'll have to talk to you.''

''Oh no, she won't. You didn't hear her tonight. And none of the neighbors have any sympathy for me. One guy threatened to call the cops on me. And I gave him a discount on a bike for his kid just last week!''

''Just for crawling around his neighbor's fire escape at midnight and yelling at a girl while he was trying to sleep? What a heartless boor.''

''Exactly. So, how do I get her to listen? She'd tear up letters, and…wait a minute, she's a businessperson, just like me.''

"Yeah, so?"

"We're also both retailers. And what's the one thing common to all retail establishments?"

"Greed?"

Nick shook his head. "No. Well, yes, but what's the one public pronouncement common to all of them?"

Gary didn't bother to try to cover his yawn this time. "I don't know. What?"

"The customer is always right."

"Ah," Gary murmured. "So, you plan to attack her at her place of business. You know, not to throw a wet blanket on your plan, but she could call a cop and get you arrested for loitering, or malicious mischief or something equally embarrassing."

Nick, the gleam of determination firmly planted in his eyes, dismissed those potential threats with an impatient wave of his hand. "I doubt it. Those sorts of things are last resorts. Besides, I'm not going to cause any scenes. I'll even make sure I never ever raise my voice."

"Are you kidding me? He stood outside your window on your fire escape?"

Meg pulled more books from the box she'd just opened and checked them against the packing list. "No, I'm not kidding. I got the machine so I wouldn't have to talk to him, but I ended up talking to him when he threatened to come over. Then, he came over anyway. Any normal human being would've gotten the message from my answering machine and left me alone."

Slicing the top off another box with a utility knife, Shawn pulled out a copy of a children's book and waved it at Meg. "You know, maybe if you'd talked to him, he wouldn't have had to come over and shout at you through your window."

"Shawn, you know what he did. How can you defend him? I poured out my innermost feelings to James and I

116 SORRY, WRONG NUMBER

practically gave my heart away to Nick, only to find out that they're the same person. When I think about all the things I told James about Nick . . . well, it's just too humiliating to think that he was laughing at me and telling all his friends what a poor miserable soul I was."

An empty box sailed toward the back door to join a pile of empty boxes. Shawn cleared her throat. "I don't want to say I told you so about the James thing, Meg, but beyond that, even though it was a rotten thing to do, maybe you should let Nick explain. Maybe it isn't quite as bad as it seems."

Meg placed the books she held on a wooden library cart and turned suspicious eyes on her assistant. "Why are you all of a sudden so open-minded about this? As I recall, last night you were almost as ticked off at Nick as I was. What's brought on this sudden change of attitude?"

Shawn tucked a stray strand of hair behind her ear and cleared her throat again. "What do you mean? I'm just trying to help you see that there might be two sides to this."

"No, you're not. You've been collaborating with the enemy, haven't you?"

Unable to withstand Meg's accusing glare, Shawn threw up her hands. "All right, so Gary called me before I left for work and asked me to talk to you. Apparently, Nick went to see him after he left your place last night. Gary said that Nick didn't mean to hurt you, but he let things get a little out of hand."

Meg thought that that was a clever way of twisting the facts to Nick's advantage. "I don't suppose that Gary knew anything about any of this the whole time it was going on?"

"Um . . . actually, he sort of . . . well, he said that he did, but—"

"See? That's exactly what I was afraid of. How could Nick have done that? And to think that I actually thought he was so wonderfully right for me. Well, I guess the joke really was on me.''

Shawn started to say something when two loud buzzes sounded from a gadget on the wall. ''I guess Marty needs some help.''

She started for the door that led into the store, then Shawn paused and looked back at Meg. ''You know, maybe it really was only a mistake in judgment on his part.''

Meg didn't say anything, and Shawn left the back room. Meg returned her concentration to unpacking the shipment of books. She tried to be more objective and think about what Shawn had said but found that her hurt was still too fresh and sharp for that. Her whole way of looking at Nick, her way of thinking about him, had shifted when she'd found out he was James. How could she just forgive and forget something like that?

She remembered most of the things she'd talked about with James, but it was impossible to remember everything. It wasn't the little things that made her want to move to Australia to avoid ever seeing Nick again. It was the times she'd confided things so personal that not even her mother knew about them. And now, Nick, the man she'd fallen in love with, knew all those things. He knew them, but he shouldn't, because she hadn't been ready to tell him. She'd wanted to wait until their relationship had grown and strengthened before risking that much of herself. Now, the thought that Nick was privy to her most private thoughts made Meg quake.

He knew that she was in love with him, because she'd told James. She hadn't told Nick, because she wasn't quite ready. Thinking about it made her want to hide. She didn't want to look into Nick's face and see the mocking look in his eyes as he remembered everything she'd told him.

That was the real reason she didn't want to see him anymore, she thought. It wasn't because she didn't love him anymore. It was because she couldn't trust him not to hurt her anymore.

Chapter Seven

It was just before noon on Monday when it started. Marty, a part-time college student, simply buzzed the back room and Meg picked up the telephone extension.

"Yes?" Meg asked.

"There's a delivery man here with something you have to sign for."

"Me? Why can't you sign for it?"

"Believe me," Marty said firmly, "you should come up."

"All right," she grumbled as she hung up the phone and pushed back her chair, heading for the door that opened into the store.

Marching up the center aisle of the store, Meg straightened books as she went, as was her habit. She spotted a uniformed delivery man leaning casually against the cash register counter.

"You Meg Porter?"

"Yes, I am. What is it that I— Oh, my gosh."

"Tell me about it, lady. Where do you want them?"

Meg just stared in stupefaction at the huge basket o
flowers. Attached to the wicker handle that stood three fee
off the floor were several balloons with various message
printed on them, the crux of which were pleas for her for
giveness. She just stared at them, as did several customer
who were already in the store, and a few more who had
come in since she'd been standing there.

"Come on, lady, I ain't got all day."

"What?" Meg looked up into the impatient face of th
deliveryman, who was holding his clipboard out to her. Sh
automatically signed it and handed it back to him.

"Do you want I should put them someplace, or just leave
them here?"

Meg's wide eyes closed momentarily as she tried to re
gain her bearings. She knew Nick had sent the flowers, bu
she wasn't sure what she thought about his doing it. She
stepped behind the counter to retrieve her purse and tipped
the deliveryman, who nodded at her and left the store. Meg
just bit her lower lip and stared at the huge arrangemen
blocking part of the main aisle.

"So, are you just going to leave them there?" Marty wa
leaning over the counter to get a closer look.

"No, I suppose not," Meg sighed. "I'll take them into th
back, I guess."

"Good idea. Some of our customers might be allergic, o
something."

Meg's eyes narrowed and slid sideways as she warned
Marty without saying a word that now was not the time fo
witticisms. She gingerly lifted the basket and lugged it down
the main aisle and into the back room. Of course, on th
way she had to endure several envious glances, several mur
murs about how lucky she was, and one jokester who
wanted to know when the funeral was.

Finding a place for them in the crowded back room wasn'
an easy chore, either. She finally just put them in the smal

bathroom and mentally dared anyone to say anything about it.

Shawn returned from her lunch break a few minutes later and breezed through the door as she made a beeline for Meg's desk.

"What's going on up front? Marty said something very cryptic about love being in the air, as well as pollen. Then two women asked me if I was engaged."

Meg swiveled in her chair and pointed at the bathroom door. "Check out the bathroom."

Confused, Shawn glanced over toward the door in the corner. "I don't have to go to the bathroom. Why are you suggesting that I do? Have you got a snake or an alligator or some other disgusting reptile in there?"

"No, I don't. Just go and look."

Shawn approached the door and opened it carefully, jumping back as she did so. After frowning at Meg's scoffing snort, she peered into the room.

"Oh, my gosh."

"My words, exactly."

"Is there a note?"

Meg picked at her cuticles. "I don't know. I didn't look."

After a moment of diligent rooting among the flowers and their stems, Shawn came out waving the small, white envelope. "Lookee, lookee."

"No, you lookee, lookee, if you like. I don't want to."

Shawn slumped dejectedly into a nearby folding chair and crossed her legs, tapping the envelope on her knee. "Come on, what harm can it do to read his little note?"

"Because I don't want to see him anymore, and I don't want to talk to him, and I don't want to read his little note."

Shawn ripped the envelope open and pulled the card out. "All right, then I will."

After she scanned the brief message, Shawn returned the card to its envelope and placed it silently on the desk between them. Meg glanced at it, then over at Shawn, who just sat there with a smirky grin on her face. When Meg made no move to pick it up, Shawn reached for the envelope.

"Since you don't want to read this, I'll just get rid of it for you."

Digging into her purse, Shawn came up with a lighter and flicked it, causing a flame to burst into life. Holding the card with her right hand, she held the flame beneath it. Just as the corner caught fire, Meg blew out the flame and snatched the card away from Shawn.

"I'll destroy it when and if *I* want to."

Shawn just grinned. "Sure. Whatever you want. I have to go relieve Marty."

Staring at the envelope after Shawn left, Meg turned it around and around in her fingers. She was more than just a little curious as to what it said. At the same time, she was wary of it. She really didn't want to see Nick again, right? So why should she care what he'd written on some note? If it weren't for the fact that she loved flowers so much, she might have tossed them, too.

Her fingers slid the card from the envelope, but her eyes refused to focus on it. She looked at the collection of paperwork, order forms, pencils, pens and stamp pads on her desk. But she knew she was just delaying the inevitable, so she let her gaze revert back to the white card she held in her hand.

The writing was masculine and brief. Bold black on stark white.

Meg,
Don't let what we have die.
We can work it out.
Talk to me.

                                                    Nick

She shoved the card back into the envelope and tossed it onto her desk.

"What nerve. *I* shouldn't let it die? Who inflicted the fatal wound? Not me. Don't you dare try to blame this on me, Nick Morgan."

Her hands came up to cover her face and she leaned back in her chair. "I've gone insane. I'm talking to a card."

The rest of the week continued to bring more and more flowers to the bookstore for Meg. There were similar cards attached to all of them. By Friday afternoon, Shawn was glancing expectantly toward the front door.

"He's late."

Meg adjusted a small display of books that sat on the counter and then glanced at Shawn. "Who's late?"

"The delivery man. With the flowers. He's late."

A soft groan escaped her, then Meg set her jaw. "He isn't late. Nick's probably just finally gotten the message that I don't want to talk to him and I don't want to see him."

"I don't think so," Shawn replied in a singsong voice, still watching the front door.

"Well, I do. It's nearly five-thirty and at six we close. Why don't we go out to eat or to a movie or something?"

Shawn looked away from the front door but didn't look directly at Meg. "Uh, I can't. I have ... a date."

"Oh." Meg started to shrug, then stopped and gave Shawn's face a closer scrutiny. "You're going out with Gary, aren't you?"

Brown eyes flashed in self-defense as Shawn squared her shoulders. "So what if I am? Just because you dumped Nick doesn't mean I can't still see Gary."

The fact that Shawn was right didn't help Meg much. She didn't want her friend going out with Nick's friend. If not exactly a betrayal, it was surely somehow unfair.

"All right," Meg finally said. "I didn't mean to get you all bristly."

Shawn nodded. "I know. But I think that if you'd just sit down and talk with Nick, you'd feel a lot better. Even if you just yell at him, face to face, you'd at least get it off your chest. The way it is now, you're just walking around with this big hurt and no way to vent it."

About to refute Shawn's argument, Meg was distracted by the sound of the front door opening.

"Good grief, they're bigger than all the rest of them," Shawn exclaimed.

Meg stared at the huge basket of flowers the deliveryman carried. They were gladiolus...probably two or three dozen of them. The tops of the flowers obscured the delivery-man's upper body. All that could be seen were a pair of jeans and sneakers and the flowers.

"I'm not giving you another tip," Meg said wearily. "I can't afford it anymore."

The man set the basket on the floor, and Meg gasped when she saw Nick's face emerge above the flowers instead of the deliveryman's.

"Well, fine, if you're going to be stingy about it. Actually, though, I really didn't expect money. Just some of your time."

"Oh, speaking of time," Shawn said pointedly. "I have to put some books away before I leave."

"Shawn," Meg warned.

"And look, there are two customers who, I'm sure, need help."

Then the traitor was gone and Meg was left standing at the edge of the cash register area with Nick and a huge basket of flowers.

"Meg," he said softly, then paused. "Do you...did you like the flowers?"

Closing her eyes against the sight of him wasn't enough. She couldn't block out the sound of his voice or the smell of his cologne. His very presence invaded her senses and made her vulnerable to him. And she didn't want that to happen again. That was why she had refused to see him.

"Yes...no...I..." She took a deep breath and opened her eyes, trying to steel herself against wanting him. "Nick, I told you I didn't want to see you, and I don't. Please leave."

"Liar," he said softly.

Meg's eyes flared with anger. "What?"

"You do want to see me. You're just being stubborn because of what you believe to be your wounded pride."

She didn't like the hollow feeling in her stomach, and Meg fought to quell it. "Well, when pride is just about all you have left, you tend to want to hang onto it."

With that, she stepped past him to grab a stack of paperback novels from the cart sitting in the aisle and proceeded to the general fiction section. Nick left the flowers blocking the aisle and followed her.

"Come on, Meg, be reasonable. I admit I was wrong to do what I did, but I swear there was no malice involved. I just handled it all wrong."

Shoving a book onto the shelf, Meg snorted. "If you think your saying you're sorry is supposed to fix everything, then you'd better sit down and do some more thinking."

"All right," he snapped. "I will. If you'll listen to what I have to say. Let me explain what happened and why I did what I did. They aren't very good, as excuses go, but they're all I have. And I don't want to lose you, Meg."

The determined sound of his voice made her hand falter slightly as she shelved the next book. "I'm afraid you've already lost me, Nick."

His hand grasped her upper arm and held her. "I refuse to believe that. Not yet. Talk to me, Meg. Have dinner with me."

"Yoo-hoo! Is anyone here?"

Meg rose on tiptoes to look over the top of the shelf unit beside them and saw a woman standing by the cash counter.

"I'll be right there." She looked at Nick's shoulder. "I have to go."

Refusing to release her, Nick persisted. "Dinner?"

Meg pulled futilely at her arm, then reluctantly looked up into his eyes. She knew she shouldn't have done it, because she saw an unwavering resolve in their hazel depths. Regardless of what she'd said she wanted, Meg knew she couldn't avoid Nick forever. Living and working in such close proximity made that impossible. Maybe if she talked with him, they could forge some sort of neighborly friendship. And the awful truth was, she missed him. She missed seeing him, talking with him . . . kissing him.

"No!"

"You don't have to yell."

Meg clamped her mouth shut. She hadn't realized that she'd spoken aloud until then. She also knew she was a sap for doing it, but she found herself agreeing to dinner with Nick.

"I didn't mean to yell. I guess it wouldn't hurt to go to dinner. But don't think it's because I think you're any less of a creep. I guess I have some things to say to you, as well."

His rueful smile nearly had her heart beating double-time. "I'm sure you do. I'll pick you up at seven."

Then he was gone and Meg hurried toward the counter to wait on the customer. She had the feeling that she was going to regret giving in to Nick. But with a resigned sigh, she knew that he would have persisted until he had gotten his way. Better to just get it over with now, rather than let it drag on. Once he saw that she wasn't just going to forgive him and pick up where they left off, maybe he'd get the message and leave her alone.

And then she would be able to forget him, right?

Meg didn't even pretend to think she could convince herself of that.

She knew she was in trouble when Nick showed up at the door to her apartment looking devastatingly handsome and carrying a single white rose. Meg gulped nervously as she took the delicate flower from his outstretched hand, and tried to put her eyes back into her head as she took in his personal statement of sartorial splendor.

A white blazer and pale gray slacks were set off by a black silk shirt and white tie. Meg didn't have to look at his feet to know that he was wearing white shoes, but she saw them anyway when she turned away to put her rose in water.

"You look beautiful."

The softly spoken words shattered a silence that Meg hadn't really known existed. Her mind had been too busy to notice that she hadn't said anything.

"Thank you." What else could she say?

She placed the rose in a slender vase and thought that with the amount of time she'd taken to get ready for this date, she should be beautiful. Disgusted with how much she cared about what he thought, she had nevertheless taken great pains with her preparations.

Her naturally wavy hair had been curled and pulled back with white combs. She wore a white sundress with red piping that crisscrossed the bodice and formed the wide straps that went over her shoulders to crisscross her back. It was a dress her mother had given her two years before but that she'd never thought she'd have the courage to wear. And she wasn't sure if it was courage or defiance that caused her to wear it now. It wasn't that it was provocative, exactly. But it did absolutely nothing to camouflage Meg's figure.

White strappy sandals were on her feet, which were now shifting the weight of her body back and forth.

"Meg?"

Realizing that she couldn't just stand there and stare at the flower any longer, Meg took a deep breath and turned to face him. "I'm ready," she said, and leaned forward to pull a white, crocheted shawl from the back of her armchair. "Where are we going?"

Nick didn't say anything until she looked into his eyes, and then he smiled slowly. "It's a surprise."

A week ago she might have teased him or wheedled him, but now she did neither. Nodding stiffly, she merely walked ahead of him and opened her apartment door. Nick followed her and waited until she'd locked the door before walking down the stairs with her.

He didn't touch her once on the trip to the street, but Meg thought he may as well have, since he walked so close to her.

At his car, he held the door open for her and took her elbow as she lowered herself onto the seat. She felt the heat of his fingers on the bare skin of her arm, then felt that heat continue up her arm and begin spreading over her chest.

When he released her and shut the door, Meg watched him walk around to the driver's side, and hated the fact that she'd felt a sudden chill when he released her arm.

"Want me to close the sun roof?"

Meg looked up at the murky sky and then at Nick, shaking her head. "No, it's fine."

"Are you sure? I wouldn't want you to get mad if the wind messes up your hair."

"It won't hurt it. Besides, I have a brush in my purse."

He nodded and started the car. Five minutes later they were nearing the Brooklyn Bridge, and Meg looked over at Nick in surprise. They were going into the city. Meg wondered what he had in mind but wasn't willing to ask him, so she just stared out the window and let her curiosity eat at her brain.

Where was he taking her? It couldn't be a really nice restaurant, because they weren't dressed for it. Same thing applied to a trendy nightclub. Maybe one of those out-of-the-way Italian places in the Village?

Nick didn't offer any hints whatsoever. Whistling casually, he switched on the car's radio and tuned in an oldies station, letting the music of Chuck Berry flow around them.

His fingers tapped a rhythm on the steering wheel and Nick suddenly leaned toward Meg and said, "Isn't this great? Riding over the Brooklyn Bridge on a summer night with the sun roof open and Chuck Berry singing 'No Particular Place to Go.'"

Meg frowned at him. "Is that a hint that we have no particular place to go? That we're just riding around in your automobile?"

He laughed. "No, we *definitely* have a particular place to go. Unfortunately, first, we have to park my automobile."

Nick surprised Meg with the swiftness of his ability to find a parking spot in New York City, then just shrugged and smiled as he turned off the ignition before he got out and closed the sun roof.

"I guess we got lucky tonight, hmm?"

Meg just mumbled something unintelligible and got out of the car. Nick joined her and before she knew it, they were turning down a street and had only walked half a block when Nick's hand tightened on her elbow and drew her to a halt.

As she looked around, Meg wondered why they'd stopped. Then she saw the modest sign on the door of the building before them. It was a theater. A very small, very off-Broadway theater, but she did recognize the name.

Nick shrugged. "I thought maybe we'd catch this show before we eat. It's supposed to be really good."

"Yes, I read the review in the *Times*."

"Did you?"

Urging her forward, Nick held open the door to the practically nonexistent lobby. An usher looked at the two tickets that Nick withdrew from his pocket and showed them to their seats.

Meg doubted that the theater had one hundred seats. Probably around seventy-five, and they were folding chairs, arranged on a series of platforms, with the stage below them.

"This building used to be a bakery," Nick said softly. "Before this group bought it and renovated it."

About to ask him how he knew so much about this theater, Meg's words halted as the lights dimmed.

The play was a comedy with only two characters and very little in the way of sets. Those considerations didn't seem to matter almost as soon as the play got under way. Meg found the characters charming and funny, and found herself relaxing a little as she watched the plot unfold.

Sometime during the first act, Nick slipped her hand into his, but Meg couldn't for the life of her recall when he'd done it. She firmly but calmly removed her hand and kept her eyes fixed on the stage the whole time.

At the intermission they got up and walked outside to stretch their legs, along with most of the other patrons.

"Pretty good show, hmm?"

Meg nodded. Small talk was safe talk. "Yes, it is. I keep forgetting that places like this are all over New York. I'm so used to the hype and publicity of the big shows on Broadway, that it's easy to lose sight of the fact that theaters like this exist, too."

"Yeah, I have a friend who's an actor. He did a couple of shows here. That's how I came to know about it."

The sound of bells chiming through the open lobby door announced that intermission was nearly over and they went back inside for the second act.

The applause, including her own, was enthusiastic at the play's end. But Meg wondered how she had been able to keep even half of her concentration on the performance when her awareness of Nick seemed to increase by measurable amounts every minute. The heat of his body, the casual touch of his hand, the scent of his cologne. Meg mentally scolded herself for being so weak as they emerged from the theater and walked down the sidewalk, Nick's hand resting gently on Meg's waist.

It took several minutes for her to realize that they were even farther away from the parked car. Then she saw the restaurant awning and noticed that other theater patrons walked near them, obviously with the same destination in mind.

"Italian," she murmured as they walked inside.

Nick leaned closer to hear her. "Yes. Italian. Don't you like Italian? We could go someplace else."

"No," she said quickly. "This is fine."

And dark. And intimate. And romantic.

Meg felt a niggle of suspicion about Nick's motivations. He'd said he wanted to talk with her. She hadn't expected an evening at the theater and dinner in a quiet restaurant with tables for two so small that her knees bumped up against Nick's when they sat down.

She smiled weakly and tried to move her knees. Nick smiled knowingly and made sure they stayed touching his.

Giving up the battle, Meg sighed and picked up her menu. She stared at the words, but even the side printed in English could have been in Italian for all the good it did her. Nick wasn't content to just have his knees touching hers.

"Stop that," she whispered.

His eyes were too innocent. "Stop what?"

Meg glared at him over the top of her menu as his knees brushed back and forth against hers.

"That," she snapped.

He looked horribly disappointed, but his knees stopped moving.

"Have you decided what you want?"

His softly voiced question caused Meg to gaze wonderingly at him. What did she want? She wanted him. She wanted him the way he was and the way they were before she'd found out he was James.

The waiter stood patiently by their table, his pencil poised. Meg cleared her throat and dropped her gaze back to her menu.

"I'll have the lasagna," she said without seeing what was actually printed. She was in an Italian restaurant, how much could she mess up ordering lasagna?

Nick smiled at her, and she knew that he could see right through her.

"I'll have the same," he said to the waiter, then added orders for wine and bread and salads. Meg set her jaw stubbornly and told herself not to let him get away with being so smug. So she was still attracted to him, so what? That didn't mean that she was just going to overlook what had happened and forget what he'd done to her.

Unfortunately for her firm resolve, delicious food, two glasses of wine and the candlelight had a soothing effect on her mood, making her decidedly mellow by the time Nick paid the check and put his arm around her waist to guide her back outside and toward his car.

"That was a really wonderful dinner, Nick," Meg said solemnly when he opened the car door for her.

He looked into her eyes and smiled. "I'm glad you enjoyed it."

"And the play was wonderful, too," she added.

He didn't say anything, but his smile deepened.

Meg leaned a little closer to him and shook her head. "But that doesn't mean that I've changed my mind about anything. You can't bribe me with dinner and a play and think I'll forgive you just like that."

"I didn't expect that," Nick insisted. "I just thought that we could spend a nice evening in the city and then we could talk. Okay?"

Meg's gaze remained narrow, but she nodded and sank into the car. It didn't take Nick long to get around the car, and soon they were headed back to Brooklyn.

When was he going to get around to the "talking" he'd told her he wanted to do? Meg wondered. So far it had been conversational and non-personal for the most part. She'd suffered through bouts of nervousness throughout the evening, never knowing when he might start to talk about the very things she didn't want to talk about, even though she knew they needed to be.

But he hadn't even attempted his "explanation," and Meg began to wonder if he'd ever intended to explain, or if he'd just been stringing her along again.

"I'm still the same person I was last week, Meg."

His voice wasn't very loud, but Meg jumped as if he'd shouted. Then she realized what he'd said. She licked her suddenly dry lips. "Are you? Maybe to yourself, you are. But to me, you're different."

After he exited the bridge, Nick steered his car toward their neighborhood. Meg glanced over at him in the darkness of the car and could see that his jaw was clenched and that his hands gripped the steering wheel too tightly.

It took another five minutes to reach their street, and Meg swore they were the longest five minutes of her life. She told herself she shouldn't have been surprised when he cut the engine and followed her up to her apartment.

Jamming the key into the lock with fingers that only shook a little, Meg left the door open and walked into her apartment, flicking lights on as she put as much distance between them as her tiny apartment allowed. She dropped her shawl onto the back of the armchair and turned to watch Nick shut her door, then place her keys on the counter in her kitchenette.

Meg's body faced Nick, but she couldn't bring herself to look into his eyes. She wasn't really sure what she was afraid of seeing there. She only knew that she hated confrontations, and that this was definitely going to be one.

She sank onto the sofa and forced herself to look up at him. Nick regarded her through cautious but seemingly patient eyes.

"So," she finally said, hoping that he would just say what he had to say and leave, but knowing he wasn't likely to do that. "You said you wanted to talk. To explain. You were persistent, and now you have your chance."

Nick's eyes narrowed and he shoved himself away from the counter he'd been leaning on to take the few steps necessary to put him directly in front of Meg.

"And you're not going to make this any easier for me, are you?"

Meg just glared at him.

Nick sighed and lowered himself into her armchair. His forearms rested on his knees and he contemplated his fingers for a moment before he looked up at Meg. "I never meant to hurt you with any of this, Meg. I hope you believe that, if nothing else."

"I'm not sure what I believe when it comes to you," she said flatly.

"Well, you can't believe that I planned it all," he shot back. "I really did have a cold and really was trying to call my sister that night."

Meg did believe that much, and she half nodded, half shrugged at him. "So? Out of the last three months, you were telling the truth one time? Doesn't make a very good case for you, I'm afraid."

"Don't try to be sarcastic, Meg," he warned. "You aren't very good at it."

"I'll get better with practice."

"No, you won't. Just let me explain."

Nick paused and looked at her, an expectant look on his face. Meg finally sighed and crossed her arms over her chest, then leaned farther back into the cushions of the sofa.

"All right," Nick began. "I had only met you once before the phone call and after that, when you and Shawn came to buy your bikes, I thought I recognized your voice, but I wasn't absolutely positive. So, yes, damn my curiosity, I called you again."

"Why didn't you just say who you were then?"

"I don't know, I guess it had something to do with how reserved you were in person and how open you were on the phone."

"That's because I thought I was talking to someone I didn't know and would never meet."

Nick rose swiftly and began to pace the small confines of her apartment. "I know that. But after a while, it bothered me that you would tell James all sorts of things that you either never told me, or that I had to drag out of you."

"James was anonymous...non-judgmental. I didn't have to worry about what he would think of me," Meg said, trying to keep her voice from rising.

"Was I judgmental?" Nick asked. "Did I ever give you reason to think that I would laugh at you or purposely try to hurt you?"

Meg felt uneasy. When had *she* become the person on trial? "No, you didn't. At least, I didn't think you would until I found out that you had been lying to me for so long. What other reason could you have for prolonging it? If it was just an elaborate practical joke on me, you've had your laugh and I'd appreciate it if you'd just leave me alone."

"It wasn't a joke!" Nick's hand slapped the back of the armchair so hard Meg jumped, her eyes wide with surprise at his outburst.

"Then why did you keep it up for so long? Why didn't you either tell me who you were or just stop calling me?"

Nick shook his head. "I told myself I should. I told Gary I should." He saw her face pale slightly, and he muttered something under his breath. "Gary doesn't know any details. No one does. Everything we said was very private to me, Meg. But I did tell Gary the bare facts . . . as, I'm sure, you told Shawn."

She couldn't very well deny that, Meg thought. "Yes, Shawn knew I talked with a mystery caller every once in a while. She thought I was crazy and should put a stop to it."

"Well, Gary was of a different mind," Nick said grimly. "He thought it presented the perfect opportunity to find out what a woman really thought instead of only what she was willing to tell."

Blushing hotly at the thought of all the things she had told him over the phone, Meg swallowed some of her fear and met Nick's eyes. "I might have expected something like that from Gary, but not from you. I thought you were different."

"So did I," he agreed, but there was an edge to his voice that Meg thought sounded more than a little frustrated.

"But then I realized that if it weren't for my talks with you as James, I wouldn't know anything about you. Why was it that you could tell James all about yourself, but I had to practically beg you for the smallest detail?"

Meg gaped at him. "I have no idea what you're talking about. We talked a lot. I told you things I've never told anyone else."

"Except James," he said softly. "You never told me one thing of a really personal nature that you hadn't already discussed with James first. How do you think that made me feel?"

"But...but that doesn't make any sense," she argued. "You *are* James."

His eyes were almost sad as he nodded. "Yes. But you didn't know that then. You even discussed our first kiss with James, and then almost didn't go through with it."

Meg's face and neck were burning with humiliation. This is what she had feared would happen since she'd found out that Nick and James were the same person. "My memories are enough to embarrass and humiliate me, thank you. I don't need you to provide details of my stupidity. In fact, if you're done with your 'explanation,' I'd appreciate it if you would go. I had hoped that since we're neighbors, we could try to be friendly, but I don't think that's possible. So I think it would be best if you leave. Leave my apartment, and leave my life."

"No."

His voice, quiet, but laced with steely determination, brought Meg's unwilling eyes to meet his unwavering gaze. "What do you mean?"

"I mean, no, I will not leave your life. I probably will leave your apartment tonight, but I won't leave you."

"Why not?" she asked desperately. "The fun's gone. I know all about it. And I don't want to see you anymore."

Nick came around the armchair and stood in front of the sofa to tower over her. "It wasn't ever for fun, Meg, and I think that, deep down, you know that much is true. And I don't believe you don't want to see me anymore. I think that's just your pride talking."

Anger flared within Meg. She could only be pushed so far, and he was right on the edge. "If it is pride, it's amazing that I have any left at all after what you did to it. And what makes you think I would want to see you anymore after all of this?''

He leaned over her and rested his hands on the back of the sofa on either side of her head. ''Because of how you react when I kiss you. And . . .''

The look of indecision on his face brought the words from her before she could think them through. ''And what?''

''And because you love me. You told me so.''

The whispered softness of his words hit Meg like the jarring of a jackhammer. ''No,'' she denied too quickly. ''I never told you that.''

That sad smile hovered at the edges of Nick's mouth. ''No, you never did. But you told James, and he told me.''

Chapter Eight

Nick wasn't sure what he expected. After the past week, though, he wouldn't have been surprised by tears, or flight or even a right hook to his jaw. But he didn't expect the chilling silence that fell between them. Meg's only reaction had been a brief wince. Now she was staring unblinkingly at his jawbone.

"I think you should leave," she said firmly.

"No," Nick sighed. "I didn't mean to say it like that."

"That you would say it at all just shows me that I didn't know you as well as I thought I did, and therefore, what I mistook for something deeper was probably just a crush. I can assure you that I'll recover. Please go."

Nick didn't like the direction in which the conversation was headed. "Meg, I never meant to hurt you. You've got to believe that."

"I believe you. All right? But your lack of malice doesn't change anything. Because I don't think you understand what I've been saying. I—I don't trust you, Nick." Her chin quivered slightly, but Nick could see that she fought to control it. "Everything I thought I knew about you was suddenly thrown out of focus when I found out you were James. I don't know what to think or how to feel anymore."

Frustrated fingers plowed through his hair, and Nick nodded slowly. This was one unholy mess he'd made for himself. He just wished he could take it back so that Meg wouldn't be hurt. But, since he couldn't take it back, maybe he could fix it. He only hoped Meg would give him the opportunity to try. "All right. I guess we'll have to go back to square one."

Meg blinked at him. "What are you talking about?"

"If you don't trust me, I'll just have to start all over again and prove to you that I am worthy of your—"

"Nick, I don't—"

"I'm not giving up on us," he said flatly. "So, either you go along with me and give me another chance, or I haunt you at work and through the mail and on your stupid answering machine."

Her expression was decidedly wary. Nick took a deep breath and held up his index finger. "One month. Give me one month. After that, if you still think I'm an untrustworthy jerk, I'll back off and leave you alone. Just one month. What do you say?"

Meg looked as if she wanted to run, but Nick knew she wouldn't. She continued to study his intent expression for a minute, then looked away.

"Nick, I don't think that you realize how difficult all this is for me. I was so embarrassed ... I still am, and I'm not good at talking about things with men. I never have been. It was different with you, but now I know that it was only because I had James, and now ... I don't."

"One month," he said. "That's all I ask."

She shook her head. "No, I don't think that's all you'll ask. What if it still doesn't work after a month? What then?"

Nick hated the cold, hard feeling that invaded his chest. "I don't know. I hope…should that happen…that we could at least be friends."

Meg didn't say anything for a minute, then a small sigh escaped her and it filled Nick with hope. Finally she shrugged and looked up at him.

"I guess we could try. Especially since we have to live and work next to each other. But, Nick…don't expect too much from me. I'm still very uncomfortable with this whole thing."

"But you'll try?"

"Yes, I'll try."

Her own words still echoed in Meg's head as she left work the next evening. Why had she let him manipulate her into giving him his way? Trudging up her stairs, Meg harrumphed to herself that it was at least in part because she believed him when he said he would haunt her if she tried to ignore him again.

And she wouldn't be completely honest if she didn't admit that she'd wanted him to put up some kind of fight. Unfortunately she had to also be honest enough to admit that she was not sure that she could learn to trust Nick again. Wanting to might not be enough.

She let herself into her apartment and tossed her purse onto the counter. Nick said he was going to call when she saw him early that morning. She hadn't seen him after that. He'd spent the day at his Queens store.

With a cursory glance at her answering machine, Meg noted that she had no messages. She scowled at her refrigerator, and had just pulled open the freezer to inventory her supply of frozen entrées when someone buzzed her from downstairs. She hurried to press the button.

"Yes?"

"It's me," Shawn chirped into the intercom. She and Shawn worked every other Saturday so neither of them was always missing the weekend. But even though Shawn was her best friend, Meg couldn't deny that she'd hoped it was Nick at her door.

Determined not to let her disappointment show through her voice, Meg extended a welcome and pushed the button that would open the front door. It was another minute before she heard the knock on her door.

"Come on in," she called from the kitchenette. "I left it open."

"Well, don't do it again."

At the sound of the masculine voice, Meg's head came out of the freezer, her dinner forgotten. "Nick. What are you doing here?"

"We came up with Shawn," he said. "And I mean it, don't ever leave your door open like that. Even when you know someone's coming up. There are a lot of crazies in this city, you know."

"Yes, I know. And I won't."

He smiled at her and Meg felt warmth flowing all the way to her toes. A warmth she hadn't felt since she'd found out Nick was James.

"Hey, what's going on? Are we going to go play or what?"

They looked over to where Gary stood in the doorway with Shawn. Both wore their Splerb Veeblie shirts.

Nick turned back to look at Meg. "We came over to see if you wanted to come and play. I know it's short notice, but I didn't even know until a few hours ago. Then I called Gary and he called Shawn. So... what do you think?"

Meg tilted her head slightly and regarded his hopeful expression. She hadn't played for almost two weeks. She hadn't even wanted to think about anything to do with Nick in the past week or so. But she'd said she would try. And playing softball with a crowd of people seemed the safest way to spend time with anyone.

"Sure, I'll play."

"Thank God," Gary said. "We haven't won a game since . . . well, since the last time you played."

Meg turned curious eyes to Nick, who shrugged. "He's right. We're a mess. Most outsiders would say that it has something to do with the lack of athletic ability we've displayed, but most of us think it's because we lost our lucky center fielder."

Suddenly uncomfortable with the intensity of his gaze, Meg looked away. Shawn stood with her arms crossed over her chest, watching them indignantly.

"If she's a good luck charm, what am I?"

"A damn fine clutch hitter," Gary stated. "Hurry up and get dressed, Meg. The game starts in less than an hour."

Meg hurried into her bathroom to change, listening all the while as Gary tried to soothe Shawn's ruffled feathers. If she didn't know Shawn better, she might have been a little concerned. But Shawn was just giving Gary a hard time, and Meg knew it. She also suspected that Nick and Gary were just being nice when they'd called her the team's lucky charm. Then she grinned at herself in the mirror behind the bathroom door. The lucky charm for a team called Splerb Veeblies? How much respect could there possibly be in such an honor?

They arrived at the ball field fifteen minutes before the game was due to begin and Meg noticed that while several players smiled at her, some of the others got a little more vocal in their pleasure at seeing her. The pitcher fell to the ground and pretended to kiss her feet.

"Oh, stop it," she laughed. "Did Nick put you all up to this?"

They all denied it vehemently.

"Actually," Gary confided, "I put them up to it. Hoping that it would put you in a good mood. Lucky charms need to be in good moods, you know."

Meg just shook her head and tossed her bag and mitt next to the bench. "What are you guys going to do if we lose today? Burn me at the stake?"

"Don't be ridiculous," Russ drawled from the other end of the bench, where he sat in his lawn chair eating tortilla chips. "If we lose, you have to be the team's love slave until the next game."

She stared at him for a moment, her mouth agape, before she finally found her voice. "And whose idea was that?"

Russ shrugged. "Mine. I just thought of it. What do you think?"

Meg shook her head at his certifiable mental machinations and pointed at the field. "I think that you'd better get your lazy buns out into left field and stop raving like a lunatic."

"Yeah, yeah," he grumbled, but Meg saw a smile lurking on his placid face. "Admit it, though. The thought intrigued you."

"You're hopeless, Russ."

"Yeah. Ain't it awful?"

Regardless of Russ's ideas, the Splerb Veeblies reigned victorious after seven innings of somewhat haphazard play. With more than ten errors on each team, Meg thought it was a wonder the umpire didn't call the game on account of incompetence.

"I knew the lucky charm would work," Gary crowed.

Meg stuffed her mitt into her bag and zipped it. "Gary, I struck out four times and dropped three fly balls."

"So? We won."

Nick chuckled and picked up his bag while taking Meg's from her. "I think that what Gary means is that it doesn't really matter how well you play, because it's your presence that brings the luck."

"Yeah, that's what I meant. Now are we going to go out and eat, or what?"

Shawn tossed his bag at him. "You ate two apples and a large bag of pretzels during the game. Not to mention the four sodas."

Gary's eyebrows rose. "Yeah, so? I'm still hungry."

"You're a bottomless pit," Shawn laughed.

"But I'm a charming bottomless pit."

Their banter had lessened a bit by the time they arrived at the diner, but with Gary around, the conversation didn't dare lag.

After dinner, Nick took Meg home while Shawn departed with Gary. The mood was less frivolous as they drove through the streets of Brooklyn Heights, but Meg didn't mind. In fact, she was glad that Nick wasn't the jokester that Gary was. She didn't think she could stand being kidded all the time.

"You're pretty quiet," Nick said as he pulled up at the curb in front of her door. "Anything wrong?"

Meg shook her head and looked into his concerned eyes. "No. I was just thinking that I'm glad you don't joke around as much as Gary. Being around him all the time would likely drive me crazy."

"Oh, he's got his serious moments," Nick assured her. "It's just that he'd rather not show them to many people. Now, me, I'm a more introspective type."

"I've noticed," Meg teased.

Nick sighed, his martyrdom obvious. Then he flung his door open and loped around the front of the car to hold the door for Meg.

"You know," he said as they climbed the stairs to her apartment, "now I know why you have such great legs. It's from climbing these stairs every day."

Meg blushed slightly and shook her head. "I don't have great legs."

"Of course you do," Nick insisted. "I've been looking at them all day. I know great legs when I see them."

Digging her keys out of the side pocket of her bag, Meg unlocked her door and flicked on the overhead light. "I have okay legs. But thank you, anyway."

"You're welcome," he said simply. "What are you doing next Saturday?"

Meg tossed her bag onto the floor next to the armchair and turned back to face Nick. "I don't know. I don't have anything planned."

"Good," he said, and kicked the door shut with his foot. "I'd like you to come with me out to my parents' house for a barbecue."

Meg's eyes grew round and she started to shake her head. "I don't know, Nick. Meeting your family...they'll think we're serious, and I don't know if I'm ready for that."

"They won't think anything we don't want them to think," he insisted. "And I want you to meet them. They're less dangerous in large crowds, which is exactly what it will be next week. The whole family gets together every year on my parents' anniversary and has a wild barbecue on the beach."

It sounded very tempting to Meg, and she didn't doubt that Nick had meant it to sound tempting. "On the beach?"

Nick nodded. "Yep. Of course, it helps that my parents live on the beach. So their backyard is where the barbecue is. It's all very casual. What do you think? Will you go?"

The setting sounded great, but Meg wasn't sure about the family angle. "I appreciate the invitation, Nick, but are you sure it's such a good idea? I mean, the thought of being surrounded on all sides by your curious relatives doesn't really sound like a relaxing way to spend my Saturday.''

"They're just people. You'll love them. They'll love you. And I'll be there.''

Meg wondered if he'd be so understanding if she'd invited him to meet her relatives. "You can't spend the whole day with me, Nick.''

"Why not?''

"Because you can't. What would everyone think?''

"They'll think I want to spend my time with a pretty girl. And they'll be right. Don't worry about what anyone will think. My family won't read anything into your being my guest. My parents have always encouraged us to bring friends to these gatherings. What do you say? It'll be fun.''

Meg thought of a number of valid reasons to avoid such a potentially stressful day with Nick's family. Regardless of what he said, she knew that his family would naturally be curious about her, and she had to admit that she was curious about them. But she had promised Nick that she would try and so she nodded.

"Okay, I'll go.''

"Good.''

"I just hope you aren't expecting too much from this.''

Nick just smiled, and Meg felt her skin grow warm. "I probably am, but that can't be helped. Now, come here.''

"Why?''

She knew why, and Nick knew she knew.

"So I can kiss you good-night.''

Her legs suddenly seemed to be made of lead. She hoped Nick would notice and come to her, but he remained where he was, waiting. Meg knew that he wanted her to make this decision without him to coax her. What he probably didn't know, Meg thought, was how very much she wanted to kiss Nick again. So she willed herself to take the few steps toward him.

Taking her in his arms, Nick surprised her by engulfing her in a bear hug. "I've missed you," he said into her hair. "I've missed holding you."

Meg leaned back and stared into his eyes. "I've missed you, too."

Then he kissed her, and Meg realized that she'd missed his kisses more than she'd dare admit to herself. Missed the way his lips slanted over hers, missed the little tingling shocks that traveled from her lips to the rest of her body.

Nick pulled away from her before Meg wanted him to pull away, but his hand still cradled her neck and jaw, and his thumb traced her lower lip, which still glistened from his kisses.

"I don't think I need to tell you how much I've missed kissing you."

Meg smiled shakily. No, he didn't need to tell her. He'd shown her. And her knees were still wobbly from it.

"I'll call you tomorrow," he said as he backed toward the door. "Are you working tomorrow?"

Her head shook slowly from side to side as Meg's tongue darted out to run along her lips, bringing in the last taste of him. "No, I'm not. But I have errands to run. I have to go shopping for food, and I have to do laundry."

"I'm only going to drop in for a few minutes tomorrow to see how my new assistant manager is doing. I have errands, as well. We'll go together. Good night." He reached behind him and opened the door.

The edges of the bath towel securely tucked around the rest of the clothes in her wicker clothes basket, Meg wondered if doing her errands and laundry with Nick was such a good idea. There was something so very personal about grocery shopping and laundry.

The sound of her buzzer startled her, even though she expected it. Nick had told her across the fire escape a few minutes ago that he would be right over. About to press the button to open the building's front door, she pulled her finger back, remembering how Nick had warned her about leaving her door open, even when she was expecting someone.

Pressing the intercom button instead, she leaned toward it. "Nick?"

"Nobody but" came his cheerful reply.

Meg pressed the button to let him in and began to gather her things. Her laundry soap was in with the clothes, her shopping list was in her purse. Dressed in a pair of faded jeans and a ratty-looking Jets sweatshirt, Meg had her hair caught up in a high ponytail. She'd given thought to dressing up for Nick, but then decided that he might as well see her looking like a grunge.

He knocked on her door and she went to it, making a production of looking through her peephole and then leaving her chain on while she perused him through a slightly opened door.

Nick was just as casually dressed as she, Meg thought as she looked him over.

"Want me to show you my birthmark?"

Meg slipped the chain off and opened the door. "That depends on where it is."

Nick winked at her, then kissed her quickly. "Maybe I should just let you find it through exploration."

That thought was more than just a little provocative, Meg thought as she cleared her throat and picked up her purse. He was wearing a red tank top and frayed cutoffs with a pair of ancient-looking tennis shoes. Wherever that birthmark was, it was no doubt in a very intimate place.

"Maybe we should get going," she said sternly.

Nick just laughed at her and picked up her clothes basket. "Okay. Whatever you say. Do you want to do the laundry first or the shopping?"

"Laundry," Meg answered as they stepped out onto her landing. She locked her door and they started down the stairs. "I don't want my frozen foods to thaw while I'm doing my laundry," she explained. "It doesn't hurt the laundry to sit around for a while."

"How do you manage this by yourself? Especially without a car?" Nick asked as he followed her down the stairs and out onto the street.

Meg shrugged as she opened the front door and held it for Nick as he walked through. "I have one of those shopping baskets on wheels. I use it to take my laundry to the launderette, then I bring it back here, unload it, and take it out again to do my grocery shopping."

Nick hoisted her laundry into his trunk, where Meg spied a duffel bag that appeared to be stuffed with his own clothes. "Sounds like a time-consuming method."

"It is," she said, sliding into his car. "Takes most of a day. But it works for me. It must be nice to have a car to haul your things around in. Where do you usually do your laundry?"

Nick twisted the key in the ignition and the engine roared to life. He popped a pair of sunglasses on his nose and turned to flash a brilliant smile at her. "I go to my parents' house. My mom does it for me."

Meg just laughed at his totally unrepentant attitude. And she could hardly blame him, either. If her parents still lived close by, she'd no doubt take advantage of their washer and dryer.

Since the launderette was only six blocks from Meg's apartment, it took them less than five minutes to get there and unload the car. Once inside, Meg was relieved to note that the place was relatively empty. There was nothing more frustrating than a crowd of people fighting for a dryer.

She spotted a nice, quiet section, and Meg started forward, her clothes basket on her hip. Nick followed her, and dropped his duffel beside her basket on the waist-high Formica counter.

"It's a good time," Meg commented. "We should be out of here in an hour and a half."

"Right." Nick watched as Meg pulled her clothes out of her basket and separated them into little piles. "What are you doing?"

She looked up at him. "I'm separating my loads."

He nodded. "Oh." He then unzipped his duffel and turned it upside down. His clothes were in a jumbled pile, except for two socks that jumped ship and landed on the floor.

"Why?"

Meg frowned. "Why what?"

"Why are you separating them? Why don't you just dump them into the washers and . . . By the way, where are those machines with the little boxes of—oh, there's one."

He was about to walk off when Meg wrapped her fingers around his muscled upper arm and stopped him. He looked down curiously as she looked up pityingly. "You really have no idea what you're doing, do you?"

"'Course I do," he said. "I'm going to get a little box of detergent."

"No," Meg said, releasing his arm. "I mean that you've never done this, have you? Washed your clothes in a launderette?"

Nick shook his head. "No, but then, I haven't washed them anywhere else, either. No, I take that back. I did wash them once, but for some reason, my mother insisted on doing them over."

"I don't wonder," Meg murmured.

"You want me to get you a little box of detergent?"

Meg sighed. "No, thank you. I brought my own." She held up a plastic canister she'd filled with detergent before she'd left. "It's too expensive to buy detergent in those little boxes."

She then proceeded to give him a brief lecture on consumer economics, but the end result was that Nick still had to buy a little box of detergent because Meg hadn't brought enough with her to do her own laundry and his, as well.

"Now," she said, when he returned with his detergent and fabric softener. "You separate the clothes and wash them according to color. Whites, lights and darks."

Nick nodded and reached out with his index finger to snag a particularly lacy bra. He let it dangle between them. "What about these? Not that I have any, but—"

Meg's face flamed as she snatched the garment away from him and shoved it under her lingerie pile. "These are delicates, and if you're going to spend the rest of the morning feeling my underwear, I'll leave now and come back later without you."

"Don't get all prickly, sweetheart. I won't touch your underwear again. Unless you're in it."

That statement, whispered into her ear, only made Meg blush more furiously than before.

"Behave," she said pointedly.

Nick sighed reluctantly. "Oh, all right. But you're taking all the fun out of this."

He planted his hands on either side of his hips on the Formica counter and hoisted himself up. Meg looked directly at a sign that read No Sitting On Counters, and then looked at Nick, who just smiled.

"Doing the laundry isn't supposed to be fun," she said briskly, continuing to separate his clothes along with her own. "Doing laundry is a chore, not a recreational activity."

"Only because that's the way you choose to look at it," Nick countered. "If you look at it as a chance to commune with your neighbors, or just to do some people watching, the whole process takes on deeper nuances."

Meg stared at him. "This is Brooklyn, New York, Nick. People don't commune with their neighbors here unless they already know them, and if you're caught staring at someone, you might regret it."

Nick just laughed. "Oh, you know what I mean. What do you usually do when you're waiting for your clothes to wash or dry?"

"I read."

"Okay. That's good. If you're alone, which you aren't now. Isn't talking with me more interesting than reading a book?"

Meg pretended to consider the matter. "Well," she said dryly, "you're certainly more unpredictable."

She turned away from his smug smile and deposited their laundry into six washing machines in the row that faced them. She then adjusted the temperature settings on each and measured the detergent into them.

"Are you paying attention to what I'm doing?"

She turned to look at Nick, who had been watching her, but Meg was practically positive he had no idea what she'd been doing.

"Yep. I'm definitely paying attention to you."

Meg's gaze narrowed on him, and she would have scolded him for prevaricating, but was too charmed by his sincerely wolfish grin. So she merely held out her hand. "Cough up your dough, bud."

Nick nodded and reached into his hip pocket. He pulled out his wallet and laid it in her outstretched hand. Meg's eyes widened, then she blinked up at him.

"I meant quarters. You know, for the machine."

"I don't have any. Isn't there a change machine in here?"

Meg nodded. "Yes."

Her hand was still outstretched, his wallet growing heavier by the second.

"I'll watch our clothes," he volunteered.

Meg brought her arm in, along with his wallet. "All right. If you're sure."

"Sure, I'm sure," he said. "What are you going to do? Run out of here with my wallet?"

"Of course not."

Nick laughed at her indignant expression. "Of course not. So go get me some change, please."

Meg went over to the machine and looked down at Nick's wallet. It somehow seemed an invasion of privacy to go into someone's wallet. Even if they had given their permission.

She opened it and pulled out a five dollar bill, then slipped it into the machine and watched as five dollars in quarters rattled into the metal receptacle. About to refold his wallet and scoop out the money, Meg hesitated, then looked down.

Nick's driver's license was in plain view through a plastic window. He'd never exactly told her how old he was, she thought, her eyes going to his birthdate. He was twenty-eight on his last birthday. Which was last week.

"What?"

Meg's stifled gasp was not heard in the noisy laundry, but inside her head she groaned. Then she remembered that his sister had been buying Nick a birthday present that day almost three weeks ago.

A ponderous frown on her brow, Meg collected the quarters and carried them back to Nick. She then proceeded to shove quarters into each machine. Finished, and all washers washing, she returned to the counter and leaned against it.

"So," Nick asked, "what do we do now?"

"Now we wait until the washing is done, so that we can put them into the dryers."

Nick leaned to his left and shoved his wallet into his back pocket. Then he leaned to his right and pulled something out of his other pocket. It was a pack of playing cards.

"Know how to play poker?"

Meg just grinned.

By the time their laundry was dry and folded, Nick owed her two hundred thousand dollars.

"I knew I should have put a limit on those stakes," he grumbled as he loaded their clean laundry into his car.

"Nah. What fun is it if you put restrictions on the amounts of the bets?"

Nick joined her in the car after slamming the trunk closed and looked at her. Meg gazed back. "What?"

"Would you have played with real money?"

Meg laughed. "No way. I'm only lucky when there's nothing at stake and I have nothing to lose."

Nick merely hummed at that and started the car.

Their next stop was the grocery store, where Meg again despaired of Nick's consumer education. She would have lectured him more, but it was too much fun to watch him, especially in the cookie aisle.

"These are my absolute favorite cookies," he declared, placing a big bag of chocolate-chip cookies in the cart.

Meg just smiled at him. He really seemed perfectly content to spend his Sunday doing laundry and shopping with her. It felt sort of nice, having someone with her as she did her errands. They didn't seem as tedious with Nick along. In fact, he made everything seem fun.

On the way back to her apartment, Meg thought again about the fact that she'd missed his birthday. Knowing that it was his own fault that she'd missed his birthday didn't quell Meg's feelings of guilt. Maybe it wasn't too late to get him something, she thought, unaware that her expression had changed as she tried to think of a suitable present.

"What are you looking so worried about?"

Caught off guard, Meg merely cleared her throat. "Um . . . I don't know. Was I? I think I was probably wondering what I should wear to that family gathering you were talking about."

Nick nodded slowly. "Right. Actually, it isn't anything to worry about. Whatever you wear, bring a swimsuit with you. And some sunscreen. And a beach towel, although we could probably lend you one. And a change of clothes in case something happens."

Meg didn't like the sound of that. "In case what happens?"

"Oh, I don't know. There'll be a lot of kids there, and they can get messy sometimes. Or you might accidentally fall in the Sound."

Not liking the sound of that, Meg pointed her finger at him. "If I 'accidentally' fall into the Sound with all my clothes on, you'd better be careful."

"Why?"

"Because I'm one of those people who believes that revenge is sweet."

Nick pursed his lips in a soundless whistle as he silently pulled the car up at her curb. He killed the engine, then turned to look at her.

"You aren't nearly as timid and unprepossessing as you let people think, are you?"

Meg shook her head. "Nope. Not by half."

"Well," he said, "I wouldn't go that far. Half is about right. Half sweetness and shyness—half passion and temptation. That's quite a combination. A potent combination."

As he drew her into his arms, Meg wondered which half he liked better.

Chapter Nine

The following Saturday morning found Meg so frustrated and nervous that she couldn't stop herself from trashing her wardrobe and her bedroom as a result.

Surveying the heap of discarded summer dresses, cotton pants, culottes and blouses, Meg groaned. "What the heck does a person wear to meet a guy's family? All six thousand of them, no doubt."

Meg still had a lot of misgivings about meeting Nick's family, especially since she wasn't sure that giving him his month was really going to work. Mainly because it wasn't just a matter of forgiving him for what he'd done. Meg had come to understand that Nick hadn't intended any maliciousness. In fact, she was sure that he was incapable of that sort of behavior.

If I knew Nick loved me as much as I love him, Meg thought, everything might be different. But he hadn't ever said that he loved her. Of course, Meg had to admit that she hadn't exactly been forthcoming with the true confessions. herself. And Meg wasn't sure where that left either of them.

She sighed and stared at the jumble of clothes around her. Summertime was not generally Meg's favorite season. Skimpy clothes drew attention not only to flaws, but to assets that Meg hadn't ever considered assets. Until she'd fallen for Nick. She frowned at the conservative—no, dull—clothes surrounding her. Did they really express who she was?

"Lord, I hope not."

But they were her, she thought. At least they used to be. She remembered the dress she'd worn when Nick had taken her to the theater. It had made her feel ... sexier, even freer and more open. Or maybe it was Nick who was making her feel like that.

Puzzling that out would take more time than she had, Meg decided. But she wasn't going to wear any of these uninspired and uninspiring clothes. Then she looked at her swimsuit. It was plain black, high-necked and racer-backed. She rarely wore it anyway, she reasoned, so it shouldn't matter that it wasn't particularly fashionable.

It shouldn't have mattered, but it did.

Meg suddenly surged to her feet and fairly flew out of her apartment. She returned an hour and a half later, carrying a shopping bag from a nearby boutique. She'd spent more money than she would have normally, but as she pulled the clothes out of the bag and snipped the tags from them, she didn't regret the expense. The swimsuit she tucked into a beach carry-all with a colorful towel and her sunscreen.

Meg bit her lip as she looked at the dress she'd bought. It had seemed like a better idea in the store, with the sales clerk telling her how great she looked in it. But Meg felt a twinge of uncertainty.

"No," she said aloud. "I'm wearing it." With that, she hurriedly stepped out of her shorts and T-shirt and into the blue-and-white candy-striped sundress with flirty wide straps that had a tendency to slip down over her shoulders. The back of the dress was elasticized and the sweetheart-shaped front had stays that supported her enough so that she didn't have to wear a bra. It was an unusual and almost wicked feeling for Meg. And she liked it.

She pulled her hair into a ponytail held by an elastic band covered with wide blue fabric. White sandals completed her outfit, and Meg was putting the finishing touches on her makeup when she heard the buzzer that told her Nick was downstairs.

With a quick last glance into the mirror, Meg tried to determine if she'd put on too much makeup. She didn't want his family to think she was phony, but neither did she want to appear pale and washed out. The buzzer sounded again.

She ran into the short hallway and pressed the intercom button. "Nick?"

"Yeah. What took you so long?"

She just buzzed him up, refusing to elaborate on what she'd been doing and why. Meg didn't think Nick would really understand her qualms. He'd already told her that the whole family gathering was casual and that there would be lots of people there who weren't immediate family. Meg wasn't worried about them. She was worried about the many people who were going to be there who *were* in the Morgan family. Would they like her? What if they didn't? And why did it matter so much to her?

Nick's brief knock brought her out of her troubled thoughts and she tried to cast them aside as she quickly looked through the peephole, and then pulled the door open.

She smiled self-consciously when he just looked at her and whistled. "You look great. Is that new?"

Meg nodded. "Yes. You don't think it's too—"

"Too what?"

"Too anything," she said.

Nick smiled. "No, it's not too. And neither are you." He stepped inside the doorway and another step put him in front of her. "You are exactly sexy enough, and sweet enough and pretty enough." He kissed her quickly and started back for the door. "But if we don't get going, we will be late enough to miss the food."

Meg hoped he was right about the dress. The fact that he thought she was all those other things made her feel more confident, but until she actually met his family, she couldn't help but be nervous.

On her way to meet Nick where he waited in the door-way, Meg reached out and picked up two large shiny silver packages from the counter. "You didn't tell me what kind of gift your parents might like, so I got them a book of Georgia O'Keefe prints from the store. I hope they like it."

Nick looked surprised. "You didn't have to get them a gift. I'm sure they aren't expecting you to."

Meg leveled a look of long-suffering patience on him. "Nick, I am not about to show up at your parents' wedding anniversary celebration without a gift for them. I don't care if they aren't expecting it. I assume most of the people coming will bring gifts?"

"Well, yeah, probably, but—"

"But nothing," Meg broke in briskly. "Now, are you ready to go?"

Nick grinned at her and nodded. "Yes, ma'am. And I'm sure they'll like the book. I just hope you didn't spend too much on it."

Meg assured him that she hadn't, but she had. The book had been expensive, even with her discount, but not so expensive that she couldn't manage it. And she had to admit to herself that the only reason it seemed expensive was that she had been saving every spare penny in order to buy her parents' house. And since her parents had to sell it now, before she was able to buy it, scrimping didn't seem as imperative.

Meg waited until they were in the car before taking the larger box and handing it to Nick.

"This is for you."

He looked surprised. "For what?"

"For your birthday," she explained. "Since I missed it."

Nick grinned. "Aw, you didn't have to do this."

"Just open it," Meg smiled, then laughed as Nick ripped his present open with the enthusiasm of a child. Then he opened the box and his eyes widened.

"It's a Mets jacket," he said, lifting the satin jacket with the Mets logo out of the box. "This is great."

"You don't already have one, do you?"

"No, I don't," he assured her, then dropped the jacket back into the box and turned to her. "Thank you," he said, and swiftly pulled her into his arms and kissed her thoroughly.

"I guess you like it, then," Meg managed a few minutes later.

Nick just smiled. "I love it, but you shouldn't have spent so much money on me."

"We'd better get going, Nick."

"And when's your birthday?"

Meg could see that determined look in his eyes again. So she just sighed. "September twelfth. Now, drive. I don't want to have to explain to your family why we're late."

Nick waggled his eyebrows. "I'll just tell them we had to stop for some serious kissing on the way."

Meg's mouth dropped open. "You'd better not, Nick Morgan."

"Of course, if you'd like to bribe me to keep my mouth shut, I'm willing to negotiate."

"Just drive," Meg ordered sternly, but her lips were already curving into a smile.

* * *

The drive out to the elder Morgans' home on Long Island Sound took them almost an hour. As they drove along, Meg couldn't help but wonder at how very different everything was this far out on the island. It was just a short distance from the city, but it was so quiet and spacious. Of course, every year it seemed that you had to go even farther to get away from the urban sprawl. The relatively unpopulated eastern end of the island might not remain that way if the developers had their way.

"Why are you so quiet?" Nick asked.

Meg turned to look at him, and shrugged. "I don't know. Just thinking. It's too bad that more of this area can't remain rustic forever. It's getting to the point where New Yorkers are having to drive hours just to get into the country."

"Yeah, I know. When my parents bought their place in Sound Beach, it was still considered pretty rural. It's less and less so every year. But since they live out on the beach in a residential area, I don't think that it'll encroach on them too much. They and their neighbors are stubborn Yankee types."

Meg's smile was teasing. "A family characteristic, obviously."

Nick just laughed.

A few minutes later they were in Sound Beach and nearing the Morgan home. Meg could hear the ocean, and with every breath she took she knew it was even nearer.

Nick didn't need to tell her when they were approaching his parents' home. Two hundred yards from the house, Meg began to hear the shrieks of children playing and the buzz of adults talking and calling to each other. The smell of hamburgers being barbecued wafted through the air with the prevailing winds and Meg felt her stomach tighten with apprehension.

The engine died and Meg's gaze slipped over the dozen or so automobiles parked in the driveway, on the street and on the lawn. She wondered how many people were here already and how many others had yet to arrive.

"Meg?"

She turned to look at him. "Yes?"

"There's no need to be nervous, you know."

"Nervous?" Her tongue was almost as dry as her lips, but she tried to moisten them anyway. "Who said anything about being nervous?"

Nick's eyes widened slightly before they crinkled up at the edges as he smiled. "No one. But you might want to unclench your hands before you break some bones."

As he got out of the car, Meg looked down to see that her hands were clenched tightly in her lap, her fingers slightly white around the edges. She forced herself to unclench them, willing herself to relax, but found the task too difficult.

Nick held the door open for her, then took her hand and helped her from the car. He rummaged in the back seat for a moment, then lifted two gifts out. One was the book she got for his parents. Looking at the other, smaller present, Meg lifted her gaze to Nick and quirked her eyebrow at him.

"Well, I'm their son. I'm expected to bring a present."

Meg just continued to stare at him. Nick sighed.

"All right, I should've talked it over with you."

"Thank you."

"But I still say that they aren't expecting anything from you and will tell you that you shouldn't have bothered."

Did all men think like Nick? Meg sighed. "Of course they'll say that. All well-mannered people say things like that. And they might even mean it. But if I hadn't gotten them something, I would have felt very out of place and very embarrassed."

"Oh."

Nick seemed to consider what she'd said. He smiled crookedly. "I'm sorry. I didn't realize how something like that could make you—anyone—feel like an outsider."

Something about the way he said that sounded strange to Meg. But before she could sort everything out, he ushered her up the walk and into the unlocked house.

The foyer was dark after the bright sunshine outside, but Meg's eyes quickly became adjusted as she followed Nick into the living room.

It was a simply decorated but elegant room with antique colonial furniture giving it a rather formal look. Meg doubted that the room was used very much by the family. A large card table had been placed against one wall to hold the couple's anniversary gifts. After they put their gifts with the others, Nick took Meg's hand and led her through the house to the kitchen.

Obviously a much used room, especially on this important day, the kitchen was filled with women. From teenagers to an elderly woman with blue hair, everyone seemed to be intent on talking to someone else, the result being that someone just walking in had no idea how anyone could understand anything anybody was saying.

"Nicky! It's about time. We were getting ready to send out a posse."

The girl who'd spotted them rushed forward and enfolded Nick in a bear hug. Not especially easy since she was just barely five feet tall and not very big around.

"Since when have I ever missed one of these get-togethers?" Nick smiled at the girl, and then looked over at Meg. "Dinah, this is Meg Porter. Meg, my cousin, Dinah Farrell."

Meg smiled at the girl, who appeared to be fifteen or sixteen, and Dinah looked curiously at Meg, then at Nick, before smiling brightly.

"Nice to meet you, Meg. Welcome to chaos on the Sound. You wouldn't happen to have brought any pickle relish, would you?"

Blinking in confusion for a moment, Meg shoved her hands into the pockets of her sundress and then sighed. "Sorry, I'm fresh out. But it's nice meeting you, too."

Dinah's laughter pealed out over the room, attracting the attention of several other women. "I think you're going to fit right in," she told Meg. "Unfortunately, that means I have to go to the store and get the relish."

His young cousin smiled beguilingly up at Nick and took his hand and squeezed it. "I don't suppose you'd be willing to let me drive your car, would you, Nicky? I'd be careful, I promise."

Nick just laughed. "No way. Trust my car to a wild speed monster with no license? I may look dumb, but it's just a disguise."

"But I have my license," Dinah protested, pulling it from the hip pocket of her cutoffs. "See? The State of New York trusts me."

"The State of New York doesn't know you like I do."

Seeing the disappointment on Dinah's face, Meg leaned closer to Nick and said, "Let her take your car, you old fuddy-duddy. Don't you remember what it was like to have a brand new license and no car to drive?"

Nick frowned at Meg and nodded. "Yes. That's why I don't want her taking my car."

"Aw, lighten up, Nicky, I'll be careful. I'll even go slower than the speed limit. And the market's only half a mile away."

"Yeah, Nicky," Meg added. "Lighten up. It isn't as if she's asking to drive it into the city."

Nick glared at both of them, and then sighed as he dug into his pocket and handed a squealing Dinah his keys. He received a resounded buss on the cheek from his cousin, who then bounded out of the kitchen, yelling that she'd be right back.

"Aren't you going to kiss me, too?"

Meg shook her head. "Not yet."

"I hope my car will be all right. If she hadn't looked so heartbroken I wouldn't have let her drive it."

A woman who looked like an older version of Dinah turned away from the nearest counter and laughed at Nick. "Sucker. Yours is the fourth car she's taken to the store to get something in the past hour."

At the look of stunned chagrin on Nick's face, Meg burst out laughing and was joined by Nick's relatives.

Bless Dinah for one thing, Meg thought. At least now I'm not as nervous about meeting Nick's family.

Perhaps that was a bit premature, Meg thought a few moments later as Nick introduced her to his aunts and cousins. She knew she'd never remember all their names, and she began to feel wary again, because despite the smiles and friendly welcomes, everyone seemed to be assessing her in some way.

She tried to tell herself that it was just her imagination, and asked if she could help them, but the women assured her that everything was under control.

The screen door in the back of the kitchen opened and another woman entered carrying a small child who was crying. One of the younger women abandoned the vegetables she was peeling and hurried over.

"Oh, he's all right," the woman assured the child's mother as she took him. "He just skinned his elbow."

As she turned away, the woman saw Nick and smiled. "So, you're here. Are you hiding, hoping you won't have to flip the burgers?"

Meg felt her stomach tighten. This was Nick's mother. She just knew it. Their eyes were exactly the same. What was she going to say that wouldn't brand her an idiot unworthy of dating this woman's son?

"Hi, Mom," Nick said, kissing his mother's cheek. "And, no, I wasn't hiding. I was waylaid by Dinah, who somehow managed to wrest my car keys from me."

"Sucker."

"That's what Aunt June called me. But I don't think I would have given in if it hadn't been for Meg being on Dinah's side. Mom, this is Meg Porter. I told you about her. Meg, my mother, Ellen Morgan."

"I'm glad to finally meet you," Meg said, though wondering what exactly Nick had told his mother about her. "Nick mentions you often."

"Not too often, I hope." His mother smiled. "I'm glad you could be here today. And don't let the crowds intimidate you. They're mostly harmless, but I wouldn't let myself get trapped by any of them or you're likely to find yourself talked to death."

At least her smile didn't feel forced anymore, Meg thought as she willed herself to relax. It was then that she realized she'd been holding on to Nick's hand. Although holding was probably a mild term for the vise grip she had on him. Nick must have felt her fingers relax because he squeezed her hand reassuringly. Releasing him self-consciously, Meg hoped that no one else had noticed.

But of course they had, she knew, when she looked up and saw his mother's still friendly gaze on them. Meg hoped all these people couldn't see how much their approval meant to her. Despite her protestations to herself that it really didn't matter if they liked her or not, Meg knew that it mattered quite a bit. Probably too much.

"Come on outside and meet the macho side of the family," Ellen said, waving them both ahead of her.

The screen door opened onto a large deck with steps on either end of it that led to the beach. From there, it was about fifty yards or so to the water of Long Island Sound lapping quietly on the sand.

"It's so beautiful here," Meg exclaimed. "You're very lucky to be able to live here."

"Yes, we are," Ellen smiled. "Although there are times when I think we were better off living in Brooklyn."

Meg suddenly realized what she'd overlooked in her nervousness about meeting Nick's family. They were all from Brooklyn, and they all sounded like they were from Brooklyn. Except for Nick, that is, and Meg knew well what his voice sounded like with that Brooklyn accent.

"This is my husband, James," Mrs. Morgan was saying.

Just the name was enough to make Meg pale slightly, but she shook hands with the man, seeing immediately what Nick would look like in twenty-five years or so. And it wasn't so bad a sight.

His hair was graying and he was a bit heavier, but James Morgan was still a very attractive man. As was his wife. In fact, none of the Morgans seemed to be less than attractive. Maybe they didn't let the ugly ones out, Meg mused.

"Mr. Morgan," she said as she released his hand, "pleased to meet you."

"Call me James," he said with a grin. "We're not too formal a family, are we, Junior?"

Nick grimaced and shook his head. "No, we aren't, Senior."

James Morgan threw back his head and roared with laughter. Obviously this teasing about their shared name was something that he enjoyed.

Meg smiled, but it wasn't a relaxed smile, and when Nick looked over at her, she knew that he knew she was thinking about him being James. Her James. His eyes seemed to bore into hers. And Meg could almost hear him saying, "I am James. I always was."

But to Meg, he wasn't. Of course, she knew that he was, but at the same time, the James she knew was no more. And Meg felt sad because of it.

"Hey, Nicky! How's the flipping arm?"

A man about Nick's age was coming up the steps of the deck, waving a long aluminum spatula.

"I don't know, Joey," Nick said, rubbing his right elbow. "I think I might have flipper's elbow."

Everyone laughed and Joey pointed his spatula at Nick. "No weaseling, brother. I'm beginning to suffer from smoke inhalation."

Nick took the spatula and the large white bib-style apron his brother handed him. "Meg, this is my brother, Joey."

Meg shook his hand and wondered if everyone in the family was still referred to by their childhood nickname. Then she decided that they probably were. It was part of what made family get-togethers so special.

"You'd better get going, Nicky," Joey warned. "I think the burgers are starting to burn."

Joey then disappeared into the house, claiming some chore that had to be done. Nick turned to Meg. "Want to be my assistant?"

Meg paused. "That depends. What does an assistant have to do?"

"Don't worry." Mr. Morgan laughed. "He won't saw you in half or anything."

Nick shook his head. "Nope. You just have to stand next to me and hold a platter. Then, when the platter's full, you bring it up here."

"Sounds simple," Meg nodded.

"Oh, it is," the elder Morgan assured her. "You just have to be careful not to get trampled by the starving horde when you show up with the food."

Meg was about to pursue that when Nick grabbed her hand and pulled her down the steps with him toward the barbecue grill, which was indeed beginning to smoke.

They made it just in time to rescue several well-done burgers. A folding table next to the grill held hamburger patties and wienies on several plates, along with buns. There was also a large platter for the finished products.

For more than an hour, Nick and Meg labored at the grill. Nick flipped and kept the charcoal at the right temperature while Meg trucked the burgers and hot dogs up to the deck where another table was set up with condiments and utensils. She wasn't trampled, but Meg understood what Mr. Morgan had meant when a swarm of children saw her coming with a load and started yelling and screaming and running toward her. If not for the intervention of several mothers, Meg would have not made her delivery.

But after an hour of smelling the sizzling meat, Meg's hunger had begun to make itself known. Making food for other people had lost its charm. And her stomach made its protests more audible.

Nick laughed. "I'm hungry, too. And with a minor bit of finesse . . ."

Spotting a cousin as he strolled past, Nick snagged him, and a minute later, Nick and Meg were running away with their own burgers, ignoring the cousin's protests of being shanghaied.

After they'd eaten, Nick asked Meg if she'd like to go down to the beach and sunbathe for a while, then go swimming.

"Sure," she smiled. "My bag is still in your car, though."

"I'll be right back," he promised, and jogged off around the side of the house.

Meg suddenly wished she'd gone with him, as several pairs of eyes gazed at her in curiosity. Dinah, fresh from another trip to the store, appeared on the deck and spotted Meg.

"Hi. I hope you're having a good time. Where's Nicky?"

"He went to get my bag out of his car."

"Going swimming?"

Meg nodded. "After we relax a bit. We just ate."

"Me, too," Dinah smiled. "Do you mind if I join you? I won't bug you or anything...just to swim. Nobody's allowed to swim alone around here."

"That's a good rule, though," Meg said.

Dinah shrugged. "I know. But most everybody else is playing volleyball or croquet or just talking."

"Well," Meg said, "you can swim with us. But like I said, it might be an hour or so before we actually go in the water."

"That's okay, since I have to change and stuff myself."

Nick appeared at her side with her bag then, and Dinah took her inside the house to a bedroom where she could change.

After she donned her new swimsuit, Meg hesitated. It wasn't a revealing swimsuit compared with what a lot of women were wearing, but for Meg...

She told herself not to be a prude, then pulled on a matching cover-up. She left her dress lying on the bed. She hoped whoever slept there wouldn't mind.

She met Dinah in the hall, and saw that the girl wore a huge Hawaiian shirt over her suit, which Meg could see, since the shirt was unbuttoned. It was a very brief bikini. Meg knew that her own suit was downright conservative alongside Dinah's.

They went outside and found Nick waiting at the edge of the beach with a blanket. He scowled at Dinah.

"I guess you're coming with us."

Dinah wasn't in the least put off. "Yes, I am. Meg said it was all right. And it isn't as if I'll put any real crimp in your style, Nicky. You can't do anything right out here, in plain view of your mother and father and everybody."

"Hey, Dinah!"

They all turned to see a teenage boy loping toward them. Dinah's face lit up.

"Randy! I thought you had to work today."

Randy reached them and smiled. "I did. But I left early. I didn't want to miss the bash."

Dinah beamed at Meg and Nick. "Randy, this is my cousin, Nicky, and his girlfriend, Meg. Randy is my boyfriend," Dinah proudly proclaimed.

They all exchanged greetings, and Meg thought it was sweet how Dinah and Randy ran back to get another blanket. Nick just sighed.

"Now we'll have the company of not one, but two teenagers."

Meg let one eyebrow arch. "So? Like Dinah said, you can't do anything right out here in plain view of everybody."

"Maybe not," Nick grumbled good-naturedly. "But I could've tried."

It didn't take Dinah and Randy long to rejoin them, and soon they were all settled on the blankets, pulling sunscreen and sunglasses out of bags.

Dinah and Randy had even brought along a radio and after promising not to play it too loud, found some music they could all agree on. They then jumped up and pulled off their outer clothes without a qualm.

On the other blanket, Meg still hadn't taken off her coverup. She looked at Nick, who was pulling his shirt over his head. Thankful for the darkness of her sunglasses, Meg angled her face away from Nick, but let her eyes remain riveted on his thoroughly masculine body.

Bicycling really must be a perfect sport, she thought, because Nick had a perfect body. Not too muscular, except for his legs, which she knew had to be solid as rocks. They looked as if they were. She longed to touch him, but didn't dare.

"Aren't you going to sunbathe?"

His sudden question startled her. She jerked her head toward him. So engrossed in watching him undress, Meg realized that she was the only one still dressed. She tried not to feel self-conscious as she rose to her knees and untied her sash.

Aware that Nick still watched her and waited, Meg quickly pulled her cover-up off and dropped it onto a corner of the blanket. Not looking at Nick, she then settled back on her heels.

When she finally got up the nerve to look over at Nick again, she saw he hadn't moved but still sat watching her. He wasn't wearing his sunglasses, and Meg could see his eyes slide over her body in appreciation.

Her suit was a shocking pink two-piece, the bottom cut high with a black waistband. The top's tank style covered and supported her well, but had a flirty zipper in the front that Meg had left almost halfway unzipped. Her rather generous cleavage was displayed with more daring than Meg had ever risked in any place, public or private.

"Your bravery is well appreciated," Nick said softly.

Blushing despite her resolve not to, Meg knew well that he remembered what she'd told him about her inhibitions. Then she paused, inwardly wondering whether she'd actually explained her fears to Nick or to James.

They're the same person, she told herself sternly, but it was no use because in Meg's mind, they still seemed separate.

Nick picked up a bottle of sunscreen and pointed at the blanket. "Lie down. I've been looking forward to this all day."

Meg hesitated just a moment before she obediently lay down on her stomach and let Nick rub the lotion into her warm skin. His touch was gentle, but firm, almost massaging, as he covered her legs and arms and the strip of skin around her midriff.

"I don't suppose you'd let me do your front, too?"

His voice sounded positively wistful, and Meg laughed. She turned over and took the bottle from his hands. "Sorry. That brave, I'm not."

Nick just smiled and lay back. "Well, I am."

By the time she'd spread the lotion over his mostly bare body, back and front, Meg was sure that the temperature had gone up, because she was decidedly warmer. She knew Nick was, too, as his swimsuit did little to conceal the evidence of his arousal. Meg certainly wasn't about to mention it, and Nick didn't, either. He merely rolled over onto his stomach with a quiet groan.

Meg spread more lotion on the front of her legs and over her chest and neck, and hoped that the stuff was waterproof, because if they had to do this all over again after swimming, she didn't think that either she or Nick would be able to stand it.

It was several hours later, when Mr. and Mrs. Morgan were opening their gifts, that Meg heard James.

James? She shook her head.

Next to her, *Nick* talked with Joey about baseball. And the more they talked, in fact, the longer they'd been here, the more Nick sounded like James.

While everyone else oohed and aahed over the presents, Meg listened to Nick talk like James. Then Joey left to get another drink, and Meg turned to Nick.

"Did you really go to classes to get rid of your accent?"

Nick looked at her in surprise, then nodded. "You remember that?"

Meg shrugged. She remembered James saying that a "friend" of his had lost his accent so that "business-types" would take him more seriously. Of course, she hadn't known at the time that the friend was Nick.

"You didn't completely lose it, though, did you?"

He smiled. "Old habits. It comes back whenever I'm with my family."

Meg tried to smile, as well. "And when you get colds."

Did he seem uncomfortable? Meg wasn't sure. Then her name was called, and Nick's parents thanked her for the beautiful book, which she really shouldn't have gone to so much trouble for. But which they loved.

Meg looked at Nick and let her smile be superior. But Nick just smiled right back at her. Then he leaned over and kissed her.

Right there in front of his parents and everybody.

Chapter Ten

It was early evening as they drove back to Brooklyn. It promised to be a beautiful summer night and Nick had opened the sunroof, but something about the balmy night air wasn't as pleasurable to Meg as it should have been. Maybe it was hearing James's voice after so long....

"You're quiet," Nick said, his voice raised above the dull roar of the wind inside the car. "Are you tired?" His attention focused on traffic for a minute as he pulled off the freeway and headed toward their neighborhood.

Meg didn't feel tired. In fact, she felt restless. She didn't really know why, and she had no idea how to explain it to Nick. She had liked meeting his family, but she knew that Nick was wrong about one thing—most of them had been more than a little curious about her, and how serious Nick was about her. And they weren't alone. Meg wanted to know how serious Nick was about her, as well. But to ask a man about his intentions seemed likely as not to be an invitation

to rejection and heartbreak to Meg. If he wanted a more serious relationship, wouldn't he tell her?

"Meg? Is something wrong?"

"What?" Meg looked back at Nick. "Wrong?"

"Yes. You seem sort of preoccupied."

"I'm sorry, I didn't realize that I—"

"Don't be sorry," Nick told her. "Just tell me what's
bothering you."

Meg hesitated. Do it, she commanded herself. Ask him
how she feels. She opened her mouth, but as Nick braked the
car at a stoplight several blocks from theirs, and looked at
her, her throat closed up and she cursed her own coward-
ice. "Nothing's wrong," she mumbled.

Frustrated at herself, Meg turned away and looked out the
window. There was a sign swaying in a metal frame just a
few yards from the curb. The lettering was clear, even in the
fading light of dusk, and Meg couldn't do much more than
stare at it. Just what she needed to see.

"Nothing? Meg, I'm not a mind reader, but I can tell that
something isn't right." He paused, then sighed. "It was my
accent, wasn't it? It bothered you hearing me sound like
James, didn't it?"

Meg shrugged. "I guess it did in a way. It was a little
weird." It still was, she thought, since he still had a trace of
his accent after being around his family all day. "But I know
that it's you, Nick. I know that James doesn't really exist."

He didn't say anything, and Meg let her gaze stray back
to the sign that beckoned to her through the window.

"Meg? What are you looking at?"

Startled, Meg automatically pointed. "Oh, uh, that sign.
It's advertising a realty open house...at my parents' house,
the one I wanted to buy."

Nick peered out at the sign. "Oh, right. It's open today
and tomorrow. I guess you want to go over there and see it,
don't you? Before it's sold."

"I suppose," Meg answered. Although the thought of her house belonging to someone else caused a hollow feeling of sadness in her chest.

The light turned green, and Nick drove to the next block and turned right. It was the street where her parents' house was located. She looked at Nick.

"Now?" There was no question that Meg wanted to see the house again . . . before it belonged to someone else. But she'd thought she would go tomorrow. "Nick, you don't have to do this. I can go tomorrow."

"Would you rather go by yourself?"

"It isn't that," Meg hurriedly assured him. "It's just that you don't have to go just because I want to say goodbye to a house. It's been a long day, and you probably have something more interesting or important to do."

"It's important to you," Nick said firmly, "so it's interesting to me."

Meg just stared at him, afraid her hope was showing. "Really?"

"Why do you sound surprised?"

"I guess I am," she confessed.

"So do you mind if I come with you?"

She quickly shook her head. "No. I'd like you to. I just didn't think you'd really want to."

"Maybe you should've asked me," Nick said softly as he stopped the car in front of the house. Meg heard the subtle rebuke in his voice and flushed. He was right, she should have asked him before assuming anything. She gazed out at the house but was aware that Nick had reached for the door handle, then paused.

"Meg? Don't you want to go in?"

She almost said no, but knew that it would have been a lie. She did want to go in. To walk through it one last time.

"I'm coming."

They got out and strode up the walk, past the lawn with the For Sale sign on it, and up the front steps. The front door was open and they walked in. Several couples were milling about, examining the woodwork and closets. Meg felt her chest tighten with resentment. These strangers didn't belong here. She and Nick were the only couple who belonged in this house.

Meg didn't realize that she hadn't moved out of the foyer until she felt Nick's hand enfold hers and squeeze it. She looked into his eyes and saw that he understood. He smiled at her and said, "Come on, and show me this house you like so much. We don't need a real estate agent."

"No, we don't," Meg said, and at that moment she knew without a doubt that she really was in love with Nick. It didn't matter what he had or hadn't done or what he might do. She would still love him.

Nick's brows drew together as he looked at her. "Meg? What is it?"

Meg blinked at him and wondered how long she'd just been standing there with a dopey expression on her face. She forced a laugh and gestured toward the living room. "Nothing's the matter. I'm just too sentimental, I guess. I know it's just a house," she said without much conviction. "And I know that it isn't even a very grand house. But to me it means more than just four walls and a roof. It's a place to shelter a family and to build a future. I know that I can still do those things in another house . . . but I wanted it to be in this house."

She wanted to add that she wished it could be with him, but the words just stuck in her throat. Another couple nodded at them as they left the house and Meg pulled Nick into the living room. "I don't think we have much time. The sign outside said this open house only lasts until seven, and it's almost that now."

They walked through the living room and two bedrooms on the first floor, then into the dining room and kitchen. Other people were leaving, but Meg could still hear others upstairs.

"What's in there?"

Meg's gaze followed Nick's gesture and she smiled. "It's the basement. My parents finished it when I was in high school so I'd have a place to entertain my friends without disturbing them too much."

"You hung out with a rowdy crowd?"

She smiled at his mock amazement. "No, but we did like to listen to music that my parents didn't care for very much. Come on, I'll show you my rec room."

Meg flipped up the light switch on the wall beside the door, then pulled the door open and descended the carpeted stairs.

"Hey, this is pretty nice," Nick said when they reached the last step.

Meg nodded. "Isn't it? Besides the paneling and carpeting, my parents put a half-bath over there and the wet bar is actually a soda fountain. I used to make the most fantastic ice cream sundaes in Brooklyn."

A pool table and pinball machine were near the soda fountain, which were across from a living room setting of two sofas and a coffee table. One wall was lined with bookshelves that were crammed with books. Nick nodded toward the books. "Are those yours?"

"Yes. My parents knew I didn't have room for them, and the people who rented the house promised to look after them."

"Looks like this was a regular haven for you."

Meg looked over at Nick and shrugged. "I suppose it was. I know I loved it. I would read or study or listen to music. I probably spent too much time down here."

"That's what you get for being an only child. With four brothers and sisters, I never spent too much time alone."

"You were lucky," Meg said. "I used to wish I had at least one brother or sister."

"Uh-oh, what's this?"

Just as Meg recognized the book Nick had pulled from the shelf, he had opened her high school yearbook and started to flip through the pages. Meg darted over and grabbed at it.

"Don't look at that!"

Nick held the book over his head and laughed. "Why not? Got a goofy, out-dated hairstyle in your picture?"

"Among other things," she said, and jumped up, her body colliding with Nick's as she reached in vain for the book. The feel of his solid body against hers made her forget the yearbook as her gaze slowly slid to his face. Her eyes widened and she caught her breath when she saw desire flare in his eyes.

"I'll have to remember the effect this book has on you," Nick teased as he tossed it onto one of the sofas and drew her into his arms.

Meg was breathless even before his lips touched hers, and as her eyes drifted shut and her arms crept up to his shoulders, she decided that she really didn't need oxygen. All she needed was Nick.

She knew something had happened, but her senses were too muddled to sort out what it was. Then Nick pulled away from her and she heard him mutter, "Uh-oh."

Meg's eyes fluttered open, but she saw nothing. It was absolutely dark. Suddenly she gasped and her hands slipped from Nick's shoulder to grip his upper arms. "Nick! The open house is over. We have to get out of here before they lock up the house."

Nick apparently agreed. "I guess they didn't know we were down here." He released her and turned around "Come on, we'll just go over to the stairs and— Ouch!"

"Watch out for the—"

"Thanks for the warning," Nick ground out.

"Feel for the furniture," Meg advised, and stuck one hand out in front of her.

"I'm doing that," Nick told her. Meg could hear his feet shuffling on the carpet as he slowly made his way across the rec room.

"Nick," Meg called as she stopped a few feet behind him and tried to get her bearings. "I think that the stairs are farther to the right. If you go too far left, you'll run into the—"

"Ouch! Dammit."

"—Pool table."

"At least now I have something to hold on to," he said.

Meg eased through the darkness until she rapped her groping fingers against the side of the pool table. Keeping her hand on it, she was able to make her way forward much more quickly. . . until she ran into Nick's back.

"Oh! Why did you stop?"

"Because I can't remember if the stairs are on the left or right from this end of the pool table."

"They're over to the right."

Again, they started their slow forward movement, and after only a half dozen cautious steps, Nick let out a sigh of relief. "Found them."

He climbed the stairs easily, then Meg heard a curse from above her. "What is it?"

"The damned door knob doesn't catch. It just spins."

"I thought they'd fixed that."

She heard some clumping, and a scraping sound, then "Where the hell is the light switch?"

Meg didn't know if she should laugh or cry. "It's on the wall . . . on the other side of the door."

The silence lasted for several seconds. Then it sounded as if Nick pounded the door with his fist. "Well, that's a fine place to put it."

He pounded the door again. "Hey! Is anybody there?"

When several seconds passed with no response, he pounded and shouted again but with no better results. Meg felt her nerves tighten at the thought of being locked in a dark basement all night with Nick. Although it wasn't an unpleasant thought. Not in the least. But it still made her nervous. "I think they left," she finally managed.

"Looks that way," Nick said as he made his way back down the stairs. If her hearing was to be trusted, he stopped only a few feet from her.

"I'm sorry, Nick. This is all my fault."

"Why is it your fault?"

His voice didn't sound angry, and Meg was reassured by it. "Because you wouldn't be here if it weren't for me."

"As I recall," he said, his voice moving away from her, maybe toward the living area, "it was my idea to come by here tonight. You didn't think I'd be interested."

For some reason, his pointed words didn't make her as uncomfortable as they had earlier. Maybe it was the darkness that boosted her confidence. "I'm sorry about that. You were right. I shouldn't have assumed anything without asking you."

"So why didn't you just ask me?"

Meg only hesitated for a moment, because it seemed that if she lost her gumption now, it might never return. "I guess I was afraid that you'd think I would be hinting about something serious if I asked you to come and see the house I wanted to buy and live in and raise my family in."

She held her breath but let it out when he didn't laugh. Nick's voice, now several feet away, sounded calm without a hint of teasing or mockery. "Something serious usual[ly] means something permanent. Do you mean that you did[n't] want me to have permanent thoughts about us?"

"No!" Meg took a step toward his voice, but was fru[s]trated, because it seemed to keep moving. "I did. I mean, [I] do. But I didn't want to be the one to bring it up."

"So you were waiting for me to bring it up first?"

Meg frowned. He'd moved again. She followed the rea[s]suring sound of his voice, taking care not to trip over t[he] furniture. And his voice *was* reassuring. Meg suddenly fe[lt] that if she didn't say everything she'd been wanting to sa[y] now, she might never get another chance. "Yes, I was wa[it]ing for you to say that you wanted us to be more serious. [I] was waiting for you to tell me..." That you love me, sh[e] finished silently.

"Did you ever think that maybe I was waiting for t[he] same thing?"

His softly spoken words reached out through the dar[k]ness toward her, and Meg's heart skipped a beat. He wa[s] right in front of her. Her voice was barely more than [a] whisper. "Nick?"

"Don't you think we've both waited long enough?"

The deep resonance of his voice seemed to envelop her [as] tightly as his arms, and Meg sent up a silent prayer. Plea[se] let him love me. "I love you, Nick. I wanted to tell you b[e]fore, but I was afraid."

"Afraid of what?"

She'd gone too far to back out now, so Meg plunge[d] ahead. "I was afraid you might not love me. But even if y[ou] don't, it won't change the fact that I still love you. I thin[k I] always will."

Almost before Meg had ended her confession, she hear[d] a soft click and she and Nick were bathed in a swath of lig[ht] coming from the bathroom just behind Nick. His hand st[ill] rested on the switch just inside the bathroom. Confused, Meg automatically started to take a step back.

"Oh, no, you don't," Nick said as he reached out and grabbed her shoulders.

He'd obviously been maneuvering her over here, and Meg wasn't sure she wanted to think about why. So she looked up at the soft light that now seemed almost garish. "I forgot about this light."

"I thought you might have. But let's not get off the subject. Look at me, Meg."

She did as he asked, albeit slowly. When her eyes finally met his, she felt a sudden jolt at the intensity of emotion she saw. She lifted one hand and let her fingers gently touch his temple. She didn't care that her voice cracked with hope. "Nick?"

"Say it again, Meg. I want to see you when you say it."

Tears gathered in her eyes, but didn't fall. Her lips trembled, but her voice was sure. "I love you, Nick."

She saw his smile just before she felt it. Gentle, yet exuberant, the kiss ended too soon. But Meg didn't really mind when she felt Nick's hands cradle her face tenderly. Her eyes fluttered open to see his eyes hungrily devouring her.

"I love you, Meg Porter. Don't ever doubt that."

Two tears slipped down her cheeks but were immediately kissed away by Nick. "Why didn't you tell me before?"

He sighed and hugged her, then led her back to one of the sofas. Just enough light from the bathroom spilled into the living area for them to see each other as they sat down. Nick kept his fingers entwined with Meg's, both resting on his knee.

"I always knew you were special, Meg, but I don't think I realized that I really loved you until you found out I was James and told me you didn't want to see me. I almost panicked at the thought of losing you. But I knew that you wouldn't believe me if I told you that I loved you."

Meg didn't argue with him. "I probably wouldn't have. I didn't trust my own feelings about you then."

"I know," Nick nodded. "And I knew that until you trusted me again, you couldn't love me enough to tell me. That's why it was so important to me to earn your trust."

Meg's laugh quavered slightly. "I'm glad you put up a fight. I may not have trusted you, but I couldn't stop loving you. I wanted to tell you so many things, but I didn't know how. I needed to know how you felt, and I was never sure."

"Meg, I took you to meet my family."

"But you said it was no big deal, that no one would think anything of it."

He looked chagrined. "I lied."

"What?"

"Well, if I'd said that my family was dying to meet the woman I'd been raving about for weeks, you wouldn't have gone."

Meg just laughed. "I probably wouldn't have. No wonder everyone seemed so curious. I thought I was just paranoid."

"They loved you."

"I loved them, too," she said. "But their love wasn't what I'd been hoping for."

Nick pushed her backward into the corner of the sofa and growled, "If I'd known that all you needed to confront and confess your feelings was a dark room, I'd have turned out the lights weeks ago."

His lips slanted over hers then, and Meg wrapped her arms around him, determined to never let go. He pulled away to look at her, and Meg almost protested until she saw the love shining in his eyes. She wanted to see it every day for the rest of her life.

"I do love you, Nick," she whispered. "But I'm glad you didn't rush me. I know that I should be more confident and assertive about my feelings...."

"Just do one thing for me," he said seriously. "Always believe that I love you. If you believe that, you'll never worry about telling me anything, Meg. Trust in my love, as I trust in yours, and there's nothing we can't say to each other."

"You really love me," she said wondrously, her fingers smoothing over his cheek.

"I really do. And I'll spend the rest of my life making sure you never forget it."

Meg pulled his head down and kissed him with all the love that had been growing inside her since she'd met Nick. Then she hugged him tightly and laughed from the sheer joy of knowing that she didn't have to hide her feelings or worry about his anymore.

"I don't think I've ever felt so free in my life, Nick."

Nick's expression became serious and he moved away from her to sit up. Meg followed suit, and waited.

"I just need to know one thing," he said.

"What?"

"Do you still miss talking to James?"

Meg's eyes widened in surprise. "Well, you know, he did have the cutest Brooklyn accent..."

"Meg," Nick warned.

"Why should I miss him, when I have him right here? I have Nick, the love of my life, and James, my favorite confidant, all in one sexy package. I have James Nicholas Morgan, Junior. I don't need anyone else. I never will."

He must have been satisfied with her answer, because he laughed and kissed her senseless again. Then he suddenly pulled away and slid off the sofa onto one knee.

"You deserve flowers and beautiful music and candlelight, but I can't wait for that. I love you, Meg. Will you marry me?"

Meg sniffed loudly and choked back the lump in her throat. "I couldn't have wished for a more romantic proposal, Nick. And I'd love to marry you."

She couldn't believe that Nick actually looked relieved. She laughed and said, "Did you really have a doubt that I'd say yes? I won't even have to hire a moving van. We can just push my things over the fire escape into your apartment."

"Actually, I was thinking that you might like to live somewhere else," he said.

Meg frowned and almost asked where when she realized what he was talking about. "Nick," she breathed, "are you sure we can afford it?"

He just laughed. "I think so. Besides, don't you know that I'd gladly do more than go into debt to make you happy? And I know that living here would make you happy."

She couldn't stop the tears that flowed freely down her cheeks to water her smile. "I'd be happy anywhere as long as you were with me."

"Well, I want both of us to be happy here. So stop crying. As soon as the real estate agent comes to unlock the house for the open house tomorrow morning, we'll tell her we want it."

Meg threw her arms around his neck and held him as tightly as she could. "I love you so much."

"I only have one request," he said seriously.

"Anything," Meg promised.

"Never, ever, talk to a wrong number again."

Meg just grinned. "I won't have to. The last one turned out to be perfectly right for me."

*   *   *   *   *

Three All-American beauties discover
love comes in all shapes and sizes!

ALL-AMERICAN SWEETHEARTS

by Laurie Paige

CARA'S BELOVED (#917)—*February*
SALLY'S BEAU (#923)—*March*
VICTORIA'S CONQUEST (#933)—*April*

A lost love, a new love and a hidden one, three *All-American Sweethearts* get their men in Paradise Falls, West Virginia. Only in America... and only from Silhouette Romance!

Silhouette
ROMANCE™

 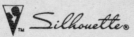